D1326420

Lilibet

The Girl who Would be Queen

Lár Leabharlann Átha Cliath
Dublin Central Library
01-2228300

Leabharlanna Poiblí Chathair Baile Átha Cliath
Dublin City Public Libraries

Lilibet

The Girl who Would be Queen

Lár Leabharlann Átha Cliath
Dublin Central Library
01-2228300

A. N. Wilson

Illustrated by Alexis Bruchon

**MANILLA
PRESS**

Published by Manilla Press,
an imprint of Bonnier Books UK
4th Floor, Victoria House
Bloomsbury Square
London
WC1B 4DA
Owned by Bonnier Books
Sveavägen 56, Stockholm, Sweden

Copyright © A. N. Wilson, 2022
Illustrations © Alexis Bruchon

All rights reserved.
No part of this publication may be reproduced,
stored or transmitted in any form by any means, electronic,
mechanical, photocopying or otherwise, without the
prior written permission of the publisher.

The right of A. N. Wilson to be identifi ed as the Author of this
work has been asserted by him in accordance with the
Copyright, Designs and Patents Act, 1988.

A CIP catalogue record for this book is
available from the British Library.

Hardback: 978–1–78658–242–3

Also available as an ebook and an audiobook

5 7 9 10 8 6 4

Typeset by IDSUK (Data Connection) Ltd
Printed and bound in Great Britain by Clays Ltd, Elcograf S.p.A.

Every reasonable effort has been made to trace copyright-holders of
material reproduced in this book, but if any have been inadvertently
overlooked the publishers would be glad to hear from them.

Manilla Press is an imprint of Bonnier Books UK
www.bonnierbooks.co.uk

Preface

The Queen died in her Platinum Jubilee Year. Even before the news came from Balmoral that she had left us, people had been reflecting, all over the Commonwealth, all over the world, not on a doctrine or a regime, but on a person, and what she is, and has been, what she stands for and what she has done.

For seventy years, Her Majesty had been the Queen. No other British monarch has been in office for such a time span. In her many speeches and public appearances, she made clear what it was she stood for and what she hoped we stood for: decency; the cultivation of simple, personal goodness; a love of all peoples, but with, perhaps, an especial love of the peoples of Scotland and of Africa; a spirit of tolerance, not hatred or rivalry, underpinned by a core belief in equality for all.

She spoke about the importance of the peoples of the world living together in amity. Visibly pious, she drew on her own personal faith to strengthen her, but she was clearly open to, and friends with, those of other faiths. She was 'above politics', not merely because she was a skilled constitutional monarch, watching political party leaders come and go. She was above politics in a much larger sense: what she stood for is so much better and so much stronger than the posturings of politicians. She was the embodiment of an idea: monarchy. She was also the demonstration of what that idea is. Other political systems are based on ideology. Monarchies focus on persons. This is subtly different from the hero worship demanded by tyrants. The Queen was a self-effacing, even a mysterious person, which is one of the ingredients of her huge success as a Head of State. Hers was no 'cult of personality'. Yet a personality was, however mysterious, visibly there. Her voice and her facial expressions were familiar to millions and millions of us.

In this momentous year, this book tries to imagine her as a person. It takes us from her birth, in a tumultuously divided and unhappy Britain in 1926, to the post-war country of 1952. It takes us to Africa, where, as a young married woman, sitting in the treetops of Kenya, she learned that she had become a monarch. The book makes the imaginative journey to discover how Lilibet, the shy, orderly, obedient young Princess of the 1940s, became Queen Elizabeth II of the modern world. It is a book about a little girl turning into an old lady, and it is a sort of dream, in which that old lady is aware of her own imminent and impending departure.

1: Jubilee Eve

I T WAS THE NIGHT BEFORE the Jubilee.

Seventy years!

The Queen had spent the evening quietly. Everyone fussed so. The children. The ladies. The doctor. Tomorrow will be so tiring. Tomorrow will wear Your Majesty out. She had obediently taken to her bed early, and asked the footman to leave Fergus and Muick in the dressing room next door, only with the door open. She liked it when they came into her bedroom to snuffle their hellos. They'd had a good dinner, bless them, some braised chicken – done the way Willow and Candy had always liked it. Poor Willow, poor Candy! What a loss to her their going had been.

And now, she lay alone. People mocked her for saying 'one' rather than 'I', but she *was* 'one'. There can only be

It was the night before the Jubilee. Seventy years! The Queen had spent the evening quietly. Everyone fussed so.

one monarch. It's not really a lonely business. She'd never been lonely, not in the way her poor sister was lonely in latter years. There was always someone around the place. Sometimes, she thought she would only be completely alone when walking the dogs! But One was One. And in the end, however much the others in the family rallied round and undertook duties on her behalf . . . well, One was One.

Perhaps she had been more tired than she had at first believed, because it was during her recitation of the evening prayer that she knew she was no longer quite awake.

Lighten our darkness, we beseech thee, O LORD, and by thy great mercy . . .

It was dark. It was very dark, dark as black velvet. And it was also light, light as the blinding light of the sun. Was she awake? Or was all this a dream? She was aware of a lightness. She had been carrying a heavy burden for years, perhaps forever, and now, as she lay there, she felt it lifting. The new sensation . . . it was freedom?

Philip was there. Not the old man who had been with her so long. Beneath the golden hair which he flopped back from his brow with a casual hand was a teenager's face. She thought it was the most beautiful face she had ever seen. He was making a joke, of course – as

3

always – but quite what the joke was . . . And Mummie was there. Well, Mummie was always there. Lilibet knew her scent, her wrap, and could hear that voice. That voice of so long ago. No one spoke like that now . . . whenever 'now' was . . . Even the ladies – the ladies-in-waiting – now sounded 'modern' by comparison. Not middle-class, quite, but certainly not like Mummie. Gawn. The days were gawn.

What had the man said, at the beginning of the reign – that man who had infuriated them all? Tweedy. They were tweedy. And her voice was like a confirmation candidate . . . A 'pain in the neck'. Philip said he'd have knocked the man's block orf, if some member of the public hadn't done it for them. But he'd been right, hadn't he, the chap who'd mocked them? Lord Altrincham, that was the name. 'A priggish schoolgirl, captain of the hockey team.'

Trouble was, they *did* all sound like figures from a vanished time. Margaret was the last whose voice had been like that. Poor Margaret. It was the voice of house parties before the First World War, of meets and balls and dinners where everyone knew everyone and everyone was related. It wasn't royal, it was class. The voice of the . . . You had to say 'class', the 'class' that Mummie belonged to.

Mummie belonged to a class. They – Lilibet herself, Papa, Grandpa England – they did not belong to a class.

They were on their own. One is One and all alone. That was what Philip had seen, that laughing teenage boy who had turned up, with his mischievous enquiring twinkle, when they visited Dartmouth that wonderful summer day when she was . . . what? Thirteen? He did not belong to a class either. Didn't belong anywhere, he said – homeless, stateless, everything-bloody-else-less.

Papa and Mummie were worried by him. Thought he was an oaf, and worried about the relations being . . . Mummie had that way of simpering and not finishing a sentence. In this case, the sentence would have ended 'German'.

And now, edging into her consciousness, here was Margaret Rose. The sad old Margaret was not here any more. Lilibet could hear her own voice scolding a little girl – Margaret Rose – who was getting above herself.

'Crawfie, tell Margaret she mustn't fidget in the Abbey. It's Papa's . . . We must all . . . after Uncle David had let them all down. After he had failed. Failed in his *duty*.'

Strange the way the faces came and went, like the flickering images on the magic lantern shows which they used to watch at Windsor during the war. For Uncle David had just come into view, so handsome, so funny. His finger had just chucked her under the chin, and he'd said, 'Little Lil.' Her chin had been aged no more than five.

But now she was ten, and Uncle David had so let them all down. And Grandpa England had gone to Heaven, and they were all in their ceremonial clothes – Mummie was about to become Queen Empress; Lil and Margaret Rose were in their ceremonial robes. They were all going to be taken to the Abbey in State coaches, and it was so important Margaret Rose wouldn't show them up by silliness or showing off. Crawfie, do tell her. And Papa, poor Papa, in his robes, waiting in the hall at Buckingham Palace, lighting up yet another Senior Service and losing his rag for the umpteenth time that morning . . . He was dressed like a King in a fairy story, with his white silk stockings and the ermine on his velvet robe, but the cigarette made him a modern person somehow.

'One day,' he had said to her – 'one day . . .' He could not speak the words. Poor Papa. She used to pray that his wretched stammer could be lifted from him. Heaven imposed such burdens.

One day? What was going to happen one day? It was all going to happen to her. The crown, that burden, that gift from Heaven, was going to be placed . . . not on Papa's head but on . . . on one.

And now, there was such lightness. In one moment, it was all happening. It was not Papa on the throne, it was her.

One afternoon lately, Sophie – such a nice girl, Sophie Wessex – had come round to watch a film in the Queen's sitting room, and she'd brought *Murder on the Orient Express*. Such a clever story – it was not a single murderer. All the suspects had done it! They came into the American tycoon's cabin one by one during the night, and lifted high the knife.

And while she was watching, she'd thought – it's like a ritual sacrifice. And then – it had made her think of something quite, quite . . . as yet another person lifted the dagger and in it went.

The Archbishop had lifted it high in the air, like a murder weapon – it was the crown. And now he was lowering it upon her own head. And she felt the weight of it. And the tottering old peers – they still spoke, most of 'em, as Mummie spoke – cried out in their Latin, 'VIVAT! VIVAT!' Live! Live! That was her duty. To live. Poor Papa had not been able to do that, but it was her duty to do it. VIVAT.

'Where did you get that hat?' Typical mischievous twinkle when Philip saw her in it. Partly as a joke to amuse the children, partly to get in practice, she had taken to wearing the thing around the corridors of BP for the few weeks before the ceremony. Papa had warned her it was heavy, and by practising, she had supposed she would become accustomed to it. But in that moment, when the Archbishop's fingers released it, and left it there on her head, the weight had felt unbearable. It is going to wobble off my head. I am going to crumple under the heaviness. I won't be able to do this. It killed Papa and it will kill me.

No, I am not. I am going to bear it. I am strong. All those feelings.

Grandpa England had known that. How had he known it? She stretched out a hand and it met his, his mottled old hand that she had held on the beach at Bognor.

But now, as they returned to her, Uncle David, Papa, Grandpa England, Mummie, poor Margaret, there were new feelings, sensations of release, as if, instead of feeling the Archbishop putting on the crown, she were taking it off; as if in the end there was a beginning; as if, as life drew to its close, it opened up like the petals of a spring flower. Not long now – though whether she meant not long until tomorrow, Jubilee Day, or not long before it was all over . . . Her mind drifted for a while into blackest velvet.

2: Birth in Bruton Street, Mayfair

THE GENTLEMAN IN THE HALL looked like what he was: a refugee from the Victorian Age. The tall silk hat, beautifully brushed and glossy, had been handed to the footman on his arrival. The rest of his attire, the black frock coat, the stiff collar, the pinstriped trousers, were what you would expect a Member of Parliament to have been wearing in the reign of Queen Victoria.

But change was abroad, and Jix, as his friends affectionately called him, did not like change. It was un-English. If anyone could hold the incoming rollers at bay, it was surely Jix. He was, after all, Home Secretary. He had opposed giving women the vote, and he and his friends, to their very great surprise, had lost that argument. At least he was able, for the time being, to limit the number of female voters to those over the age of thirty.

And at least he could do his best to stop them reading filth. He might have failed to prevent women bothering their heads with voting, but he had it in his power to cleanse the rot of modern literature. D.H. Lawrence – save the mark. Jix was assiduous in nosing out, and prosecuting, salacious literature. Why, that woman Radclyffe Hall! She had written of a 'love' which makes you shudder.

As well as banning her novel, and those of that Lawrence fella, Jix had successfully instructed the Metropolitan Police to occupy and close down some notorious nightclubs. At one such establishment, the police had been embarrassed to inform him that they had encountered no less a person than the Prince of Wales. Even more shocking than the royal presence in such a 'low dive' (as Jix was informed they were known in America) was the fact that the Prince of Wales had been found to be wearing not the starched shirt front and a white tie which any gentleman would have been wearing had he chosen to stay up to a literally ungodly hour, but ... but ... a soft silk shirt. In the evening! When the head of the Metropolitan Police told Jix this story, the Home Secretary could scarcely believe his ears. When you hear something like that, the first person you pity is the man's mother. A soft shirt in the evening! Poor Queen Mary. After all the sacrifices she had made for the Empire.

Not that Jix had ever been to a nightclub himself. They were one of the many innovations gnawing at the heart of civilization as he understood it. For Jix – Sir William Joynson-Hicks – Home Secretary, and half-successful stemmer of unwelcome historical tides, there were too many assaults being attempted on what made Britain British: who but an American would consider starting a 'nightclub'?

Worse than the sleazy morals of novelists and nightclub proprietors, was the march of the Reds. Less than a decade ago, the Bolsheviks had murdered the Russian Royal Family. And now – in Britain – in Jix's Britain, the good old Britain of silk hats and frock coats and the Book of Common Prayer – what was happening, at that very moment, as he sat in Lord Strathmore's marble hall, and heard the reassuring ticking of the long-case clock? A General Strike! The working classes united against the established order.

Jix had been inspired by the way in which so many public-school-educated, sensible young men had volunteered in the last few days as strike breakers. They had driven trains and buses, they had defied picket lines in factories and printing presses. They had volunteered as mounted policemen. No one, however, was going to forget this week in a hurry. It was as if Britain was at war with itself.

Only eight years before, the British had all pulled together, in the battlefields of Flanders and Northern France. Joynson-Hicks had been astonished, during the last week, to hear Bolshevik voices claiming that the gallant struggle, put up by a united front of officers and men, during the Great War had been a fight in vain; astounded at the wicked idea that the working classes had not wanted to fight. And when they came back, the brave Tommies, they had found a land fit for heroes, no?

A figure was leaning over Joynson-Hicks as he sat in the hall chair. Important as his reveries were – about the General Strike, about the mounting waves of anarchy and decadence – there was a matter here, at 17 Bruton Street, which was of even greater significance. It was an event which could, potentially, put an end to the march of time – stop all this madness of soft evening shirts, Communism and women's rights. That was, after all, the Home Secretary's reason, in the middle of a General Strike, for sitting in the hall of the Earl of Strathmore's town house on the very edge of Berkeley Square.

The polite, hovering figure was not the footman who had taken his silk hat. This time, it was His Lordship's butler, no less.

Jix started.

'Has it . . . has he . . . Has Her Royal Highness . . .'

'No, sir, no news as yet to report. But His Lordship was wondering whether you would not feel more comfortable waiting in the library.'

'I must stay here,' said Jix. 'I am, as it were – in earshot.'

'His Lordship' – the butler suppressed a lugubrious Caledonian chuckle – 'assures you there are no warming pans on the landing.'

'I am sorry, but there you have the advantage of me.'

'His Lordship wished to assure the Home Secretary that no one was going to smuggle a baby into the Duchess's room in a . . .'

'In a what? Smuggle a baby? What on earth are you talking about, man?'

Jix was not known for his sense of irony.

True, ever since the Jacobite times (and, as far as Jix was concerned, the Roman Catholics, *capable de tout*, were probably as dangerous in their own day as the Communists were in this the year of grace 1926), the Home Secretary had been present at the birth of royal babies. Queen Victoria, of course, God bless Her, had put a stop to the Home Secretary actually being in the room when the birth took place, although he was expected to wait outside. But it was still considered not merely respectful but, ahem . . . appropriate, that the birth into the world of a royal heir should happen within the respectable proximity of a man in a frock coat and pinstriped trousers.

From where he sat in the hall, Joynson-Hicks could look up the stone staircase, the grey walls hung with portraits in gilt frames of Lyonses and Boweses and Bowes-Lyonses, the Earl's forebears, and the eye could follow the swooping bannisters to the first-floor landing where, in a bedroom easily within earshot, the Duchess of York was confined. It was her first child. It was to be the third grandchild of His Majesty George V, King Emperor, but it would be the heir presumptive. Unless or until the Prince of Wales were to abandon his wild courses and his nightclubs and find a respectable wife, this child could one day inherit the throne. Highly unlikely, of course. The Prince of Wales was a healthy young man, who would surely come to his senses, or have some sense knocked into him by His Majesty. And he would in any case live another forty years at least. Putting jazz bands and silk shirts and nightclubs behind him, he would marry, and become respectable, and do his duty to the Empire. Surely? It was the gravest of historical misfortunes that so many of the eligible Protestant Princesses and Grand Duchesses were, ahem, Germans, but if necessary, Jix and his fellow Tories felt they might find a bride for him among the daughters of the British aristocracy.

The eye of Jix fell on the array of Bowes-Lyonses in hall and staircase. That, after all, is what Queen Mary had done for the Duke of York – Bertie as they all called him. A nice, quiet, kindly naval officer. Pity about the stammer. They could scarcely have married Bertie to a German so soon after the war, so they had lighted upon the Earl of Strathmore's daughter, Elizabeth Bowes-Lyon, and it was she who was now upstairs with her midwife, bringing a Prince, a royal heir, into the world. Bertie, of course, was only a younger son, and there was probably no chance that the baby being born would ever . . . But what is this? . . . on the landing, a nurse in a starched white cap has approached a footman, and a footman has spoken to Mr McKay, the humorous butler, and now, at a stately pace and with surprisingly swift balletic steps, the butler is descending the stone stairs.

'His Lordship wanted you to know, sir, that they have given an anaesthetic to the Duchess.'

'Indeed? Is that, ahem . . . normal?'

'A certain line of treatment has been decided upon, sir.'

'Indeed?'

It did not immediately occur to him that delivery by Caesarean section was conveyed by the phrase. When the information sank in, the Home Secretary instinctively thought of 'Macduff was from his mother's womb

15

untimely ripp'd'. Shakespeare could be very coarse and Jix had often felt that Dr Bowdler's emendations made the national poet's output much more palatable.

'So, sir, you are not going to hear anything, either in the hall or in the library. And His Lordship was hopeful . . .'

In that event, Jix was most grateful to His Lordship and allowed himself to make a stately progress to the library, where a fire was still glowing, and where he acceded to the butler's suggestion that he partook of a wee dram.

At two-forty the butler returned.

'Mr Joynson-Hicks, sir. I am happy to inform you that—'

'A Prince! We have a Prince.'

Jix had only intended to speak, but he found his voice had changed to a hoot, almost a hallelujah. It was met by the quiet irony of a Scottish butler coughing gently.

'Ahem . . . Sir, not exactly, not in so many words, sir.'

3: 145 Piccadilly

ANNE GLENCONNER, ONE OF THE maids of honour at the Coronation and such a friend, once made the Queen hoot with a story of someone, a relation of her mother's (the Countess of Leicester), asking if she could park her children with Anne and her sisters during the war. After all, at Holkham Hall, in Norfolk, where Anne grew up, there was a large nursery staff. But Lady Leicester had said that while she would be only too happy to have accommodated the children in peacetime, they could not possibly, not during the war. The friend had to understand that the nursery footman had been called up. And how could a nursery be expected to function without a footman? Anne and her siblings had been sent to their great-aunt, Lady Airlie, at Cortachy Castle, for the war.

Mummie had probably grown up with a nursery footman, at Glamis and St Paul's Walden Bury, and at 17 Bruton Street. But although there was a footman who could have been described as a 'nursery footman' at 145 Piccadilly – where Lilibet grew up – he had other duties. There simply wasn't room at 145 for a staff the size of one of the old aristocratic households, such as Holkham or Glamis. All Lilibet's memories of early childhood were of a simple, no-nonsense world; she remembered only the women, all devoted to looking after her – and, of course, Margaret too, when she was eventually born.

There was Allah, their nurse, and two nurserymaids, one of whom was the beloved Bobo, Margaret MacDonald, who would stay with her for sixty-seven years, and eventually, of course, there was Crawfie, who gave one one's lessons. The first time Crawfie and she had met, this raw-boned lady had put her head round the Little Princess's bedroom door. Lilibet was sitting up in bed with her dressing-gown cord ties, like reins, looped round the bedposts.

'Do you usually drive in bed?' the lady asked.

'Why have you got no hair?' Lilibet had asked – since Miss Crawford had what they called an Eton crop. 'Yes, I drive my horses twice round the park before going to sleep. Gee up!'

Later, when she knew her better, and had become her governess, 'Crawfie,' Lilibet had said, 'you must pretend to be impatient. Paw the ground a bit.'

She wasn't a bad horse, when she learned how to whinny, Crawfie. But not as much fun as a real horse.

From the windows of 145, they could see the horses exercising on Rotten Row. Horses were still used as beasts of burden in those days. Tired old dray horses pulled the milk-carts of Lord Rayleigh's Dairy. The coal was delivered in a horse-drawn cart. The groceries, some of them, were pulled by horse.

One Sunday, Lilibet had said to Crawfie, as they watched the horses cantering on Rotten Row, 'If I am ever Queen, I shall make it a law that no one is allowed to ride on a Sunday. Horses deserve a rest, just as much as people.'

If I am ever Queen . . .

When King George V and Queen Mary came to tea at 145, His Majesty said, 'Dear Little Lilibet – first thing I do after my breakfast in the morning. Light a cigarette – then stand by the window and look out with m' binoculars. I can just see the upstairs windows of this house from Buckingham Palace. So will you wave from the window every morning at half past nine?'

'Yes, Grandpa.'

'Dear Little Lilibet – will you wave from the window
every morning at half past nine?'

She called him Grandpa England.

There was always something very special about the bond between them, those two.

Grandpa England.

* * *

It had come to her very early, certainly before it ever occurred to her that one was 'one', still less 'the one'. There must have been others there in Bognor – Allah, calling for her not to go too near the sea – and Katta, the nursery maid, who made her dolls dance before bedtime . . . Or the other two nurserymaids, the MacDonald girls, Bobo and her sister Ruby. Perhaps Mummie was there too, but in this lantern show of memory, it was just the two of them on the shore – her and Grandpa England. She loved his great blue eyes, looking so intently into hers. She loved his grey beard and his gruff voice.

'You must never kiss Grandpa England if you've got a cold.'

'Why not, Allah?'

'We don't want anything to happen to him, do we?'

'What could happen?'

'Well, it's all right you getting a snuffle, now and then, but if your Grandpa . . . well, he has his chest.'

'I've got a chest.'

'But he's been poorly. We don't want him to go and . . . well, we don't want anything to *happen* to him, do we?'

'Perhaps not.'

'So, you promise.'

But none of this was in the memory of the beach. Someone must have kissed him, though, since the King caught a cold, and it became serious, and for what seemed like forever, the house in London, 145 Piccadilly, was sad and quiet. And then they heard that he was better and had gone to recuperate beside the seaside.

That was why they went to Bognor. His recovery was slow, and he was sad – always sad, someone said, except when he was with Lilibet. So off to Bognor! And that was why the memory was clear as a photograph. It was just her and Grandpa England.

In her nursery at 145 – when they were at home in London – she would ask Allah if she could stand on a chair. She could just see across Piccadilly and Green Park, and there would be lights on in Buckingham Palace.

* * *

But now they were not in London. They were in Bognor. They went to Bognor because no one would want anything to happen to Grandpa. That would be terrible. Things happened to other people, apparently. And, when Katta was about, things were always happening to the dolls – oh, the scrapes they got up to, and the screams they let out! Allah said they should be ashamed of themselves. But nothing must happen to Grandpa.

And so it was simply the two of them, the old man with his grey beard and his bright blue eyes, and the girl on the beach, with her bucket and spade. She remembered what Allah used to say when the nursery footman brought in the breakfast things – 'You need feeding up, my girl.'

If they were going to stop anything happening to Grandpa England, he definitely needed feeding up. Lilibet had spent the time on the beach preparing it for him, and now she advanced on him, as he stood there, holding his cigar and coughing and growling like an old bear.

'Please, Grandpa.'

'Hello, my dear, what have we here?'

'Please try my sand and apple pie.'

Why were the big blue eyes filling with tears and rolling down his old beard?

That was the memory. Cries of seagulls overhead, and Bognor, and Grandpa England . . . Well, grown-ups did not cry, of course, especially not Grandpa, who was King Emperor; it was the smoke which had got in his eyes, like it did at picnics, but he ought to have tried some of the sand and apple pie to be on the safe side.

* * *

The other grandparents were grander, somehow, than Grandpa England. Talking to Grandpa England was like talking to Bobo. He was a simple person. But the other grandparents, Mummie's parents, were grand, as Mummie was.

Her first memory of Scotland – it can't have been the first time she went to Scotland, but it stayed as the first memory – was of sitting around waiting. Waiting, waiting, waiting, that summer at Glamis.

'What are we waiting for, Allah?'

'You'll see. Keep watching the sky and you'll see a stork fly over with something in his beak.'

She could hear them all talking. They were not going over to Balmoral, not this summer. The King was better, but he was still frail, and it was thought better he stayed at Sandringham with the Queen. So they – Mummie, Papa, Allah, the MacDonalds – had come to Glamis.

Mr Clynes was there. Jix had not lasted.

'Who was Jix, Allah?'

'He was Home Secretary when you were born, young lady, but now it's Mr Clynes, and he's brought Mr Boyd, and they'll have to wait until You Know What.'

'But I don't know what, Allah. Is it when the stork arrives with something in his beak?'

The two men from London sat about in the hall in their London clothes – pinstriped trousers and black frock coats – while Grandpapa Strathmore led his other guests out shooting each day.

'Mummie isn't ill, is she, Allah?'

'Not ill, no. Only, we'll all be glad when it's all over.'

'When what's all over?'

'Well, when the baby has arrived.'

'Is Mr Clynes the doctor?'

'Home Secretary. He has to be here.'

She had not asked too many questions. Mr Clynes had to be here and they all had to be here, and at Glamis you felt everything happened because it had to happen, from the first arrival in the nursery of the parlour maid to lay the fire, to the coming of the nursery footman with the breakfast tray, to Ruby or Bobo with the clothes, and to Allah or Katta helping her to dress.

'Only, Allah . . .'

'What, my angel?'

'Only, nothing is going to happen to Mummie, is it?'

'Bless you, no. Nothing will ever happen to her. Chance'd be a fine thing.'

Mr Clynes and Mr Boyd seemed almost to have become part of the furniture. They were always in the hall when Allah took her out for her walk in the gardens, consulting their pocket watches and asking the butler, Mr McKay, whether he considered it possible they could risk going for luncheon with Lady Airlie who had been gracious enough to invite them.

'We could always telephone you, sir, if Her Royal Highness . . .' Mr McKay coughed discreetly.

'And how long would it take us to come back from Lady Airlie's?'

'Oh, she lives very nearby, sir. You could easily be back in an hour.'

Sometimes, they did risk luncheon or dinner with the Airlies, or with some of the other grand Scottish neighbours. But mostly, when Allah and Lilibet came back from their walks in the rainy shrubbery, the two gentlemen from London would still be waiting there, looking at their watches, or shaking their newspapers, as if they could rattle some interest out of them which had not been immediately apparent on the page.

And then, at last! The baby came.

'Have we got a Prince?'

That was what Mr Clynes asked, when the nurse came running out onto the landing and down the main staircase to tell him the news.

'Another Princess, sir.'

* * *

And so Margaret came into the world. Margaret Rose.

4: Childhood Scenes

THE QUEEN AWOKE, OR HALF-AWOKE.

The bedroom curtains were so very thick that the room was still quite, quite black. In that deep darkness, when one was tired, and the mind was moving back and back through childhood, it was difficult to know whether one was awake or asleep.

Where did the bad dreams come from? God sending one a ticking-off, Margaret used to say. Gawd sending one a ticking orf.

This was a recurrent dream. She and Margaret, still little shrimps, would crawl into the Little House – Y Bwthyn Bach – which the people of Wales gave for her sixth birthday in 1932. It was put up in the grounds of Royal Lodge, Windsor.

'Follow me, Lilibet,' Margaret was saying, and they crawled in and were soon merrily at work in the kitchen, pretending to wash up the dolls' cups and saucers. There was no furniture in the Little House so all the kitchen was just imaginary. As they worked, they sang – Margaret so clever, always, at remembering songs.

Nobody near us to see us or hear us
No friends or relations
On weekend vacations
We won't have it known
That we own a telephone, dear
Day will break and I'll wake
And start to bake a sugar cake
For you to take for all the boys to see
We will raise a family
A boy for you
And a girl for me
Can't you see how happy we would be
Picture you upon my knee
Just tea for two
And two for tea
Just me for you
And you for me alone

Only, as they sang, the kitchen was becoming cramped, and they were not little children any more. The house was too small for them, nightmarishly too small, and they were going to be squashed by it unless they could crawl out.

Mummie was outside, extending a hand, and trying to pull. Lilibet got out first, gasping for air, but they were still pulling at Margaret. And as they pulled, they realized that the little girl who had crawled into the Little House was now an old lady in a fur coat, smelling of Benson & Hedges and Famous Grouse. It was an awful effort, getting her out and into the wheelchair.

Oh dear. Was this what had become of those two little girls? And as she gasped and puffed and held poor old Margaret's hand, she opened her eyes in the blackness and realized she was, sort of, awake, and the bad dream began to recede.

Strange to have bad dreams about the Little House, because when it had arrived, and those kind workmen had erected it in the grounds of Royal Lodge, she had been so pleased. Her very own real little house of bricks and mortar, with a kitchen where they could play at being like ordinary people. The only trouble – no stables! So all her horses-on-wheels stayed behind in 145 Piccadilly, where they were stabled on the top-floor landing.

They had been so very, very lucky, the girls, to have enjoyed their childhood well away from publicity, living with Mummie and Papa in Piccadilly, more or less at Hyde Park Corner. Walks across Hyde Park to J.M. Barrie's house in Bayswater, where the author would read *Peter Pan* aloud to them in his lovely Scottish voice. Whizzing round the Circle Line with Crawfie – no one recognized them! (That had been Margaret's idea.) Waving each morning through the window at half past nine, knowing that Grandpa England was looking acrawss from BP. Playing cowboys and Indians in the shrubbery of Hamilton Place.

'There's Mrs Happy.'

'And Miss Woggs.'

'Children!' Crawfie had exclaimed in amazement. 'How do you know the names of all the people walking in Hamilton Place?' But of course, they didn't know the people's names – Woggs and Happy and Snuffles ('There goes old Mr Snuffles') were the names of these people's *dogs*.

Apart from Allah and Crawfie and Bobo, most of those they knew were family – Queen Mary or the Countess of Strathmore coming to tea. Their cousins, George and Gerald Lascelles, a bit older than they were, playing. The rainy afternoons with jigsaw puzzles. *The Children's*

Newspaper. Comic strips – 'Pip, Squeak and Wilfred', 'Mutt and Jeff'. 'Li'l Abner'. The joy of seeing animated cartoons at the cinema in BP – the figure referred to by Grandpa England as 'That Damned Mouse'. The simplicity of it all! Lilibet had pocket money of a shilling a week until she was fourteen. Margaret never had pocket money – quite sensibly, in a way, because what would they ever have spent it on?

Once, Crawfie took them to the YMCA in Bloomsbury. They went on the tube, and got out at Tottenham Court Road. No one recognized them. The YMCA people had been warned, of course, but no fuss was made, as far as one could recall. One fetched one's own tea and bread and butter at a chromium counter. Such very thick cups! Crawfie had to go back and fetch the teapot – Lilibet had left it on the counter. 'If you want it, you must come and FETCH IT!' the lady at the counter had bawled. No curtsying or anything. When Mummie heard, she said it was the limit, and the woman must have been a Red.

Lilibet liked the fact they did not stand on ceremony. Only at Glamis, really, when they went for their annual Scottish holiday, were they shown deference. Papa was 'only' the Duke of York, and all the public interest was in Uncle David – so handsome, so debonair, so raffish. Both girls adored him. He was so funny. He liked films, which he called movies, and he and Mummie liked making 'movies' on the lawn of Royal Lodge. He could always make them laugh. Papa made them laugh, of course, when they played Hands, Knees and Boomps-a-Daisy, but Uncle David brought a whiff of the great world. Uncle David had actually met all the stars they had only seen in the films – movies, sorry! He'd been the guest of a grand family and stayed in the same house as Fred Astaire and Ginger Rogers! He and Margaret had pretended to be tap dancers.

One day, Mummie said, Uncle David would eventually settle down and find a wife. He would have babies. He would be the King of England, and they would in turn become Kings. And Mummie and Papa and Margaret and Lilibet could go on with their quiet, happy existence. We Four, riding, and walking the dogs, and having their own very special private lives.

5: Abdication

L ATER, OH, SO MUCH LATER, they had brought her
that book about her grandfather. By now, it was
strange. Her family had become two things.
First, it was the collection of those she had known and,
for the most part, loved, the people one spent summers
and Christmases with at Balmoral and Sandringham, the
people inside one's head. But it had also been something
else. It was something she read about, in newspapers and
books. And – one thought – are these things true? Are these
people, described in this article, or in this book, really the
grandparents, or cousins, one thought one knew?

When Lilibet had been a teenager and a young woman,
Queen Mary had helped her so much, to prepare herself
for what was in store. She had taught her about the
constitutional monarchy, what it was, why it was such

a delicate, beautiful thing, like the most exquisite piece of jewellery, held together by tiny golden chains. But she had not explained to her what it would be like to read about the family as if they were characters in books, in history – which, of course, they were.

It was always a shock to realize this. Perhaps it was because she was not a great reader, but she always found it worrying, painful even, when the author was trying to be kind. To find oneself a character in a book – like, oh, she could not think of an example, *Black Beauty*, say, or those immensely brave animals in *The Incredible Journey* (one of the few storybooks she had actually enjoyed as a grown-up).

This book, though, had been written by one of those journalists Mummie knew. Someone on the *Telegraph*. She would not repeat what Philip thought about the chap, but Mummie said he was all right, and one shouldn't listen to Philip, who called him Castrol 7 ('You could oil a lorry with him'). And in the book, which was a biography of Grandpa England, there was something a proper friend of Mummie's had heard Grandpa once say – 'I pray to God my eldest son will never marry and have children, and that nothing will come between Bertie and Lilibet and the throne.'

You might have thought it was idle tittle-tattle, but Mummie had said – when Lilibet, as Queen, had wondered how true this could have been – 'Oh, no, darling. I remember when you were so tiny, and you went down to see the King at Bognor. Everyone had thought he was going to die, and when we came in to see him, he said, "David will never take over from me." We did not know what he meant.'

You could tell that Mummie still thought it was all a bit strange. But one had always known. He had known. Grandpa. It was a strange secret between them, perhaps.

That moment on the beach at Bognor. Looking out of his window in Buckingham Palace and across Green Park to 145, he had known. Accepting her 'sand and apple pie', he had known.

She'd often thought it must be so strange for all the clever, complicated and perhaps rather unhappy people who do not believe in God!

Lying there in the dark, wide awake by now, she repeated, as she did every day of her life, some of the familiar phrases – 'unto whom all hearts be open, all desires known, and from whom no secrets are hid . . . whose Kingdom is everlasting and power infinite . . . so rule the heart of Elizabeth thy Servant, that in all her thoughts, words and works, she may ever seek thy honour and glory . . .'

Like Grandpa, she too had always known. It was something which was going to happen, that was all. It was not planned by her, or by her grandfather, but it was planned. Meant. People wrote in the newspapers, when she began to grow old, that she had shown such a sense of duty. But it had not been like that. Not in the sense of trying to be good. It was simply something given to her. It was meant. It was in the scheme of things. She had quietly accepted it, as something which she, and only she, had been called out to do. She remembered Crawfie reading the Bible to her in that lovely Scottish lilt. The story of the voice calling the Infant Samuel. The little boy had kept running from his nursery into the room of old Samuel the priest – 'Here am I, for thou didst call me.' And then Samuel had realized who had been calling, and he had told the child, simply say, when you hear the voice, 'Speak, Lord, for thy servant heareth.' That was what it had been like for her. Always.

*   *   *

This had not stopped it being a terrible sadness, that day – she was just ten – when the news came to Royal Lodge. Grandpa England was dead. The shock was terrible.

'So, is Uncle David the King?'

'When you see him, you must curtsey.'

Margaret had said, 'King David! It's like the Bible.'

And Mummie had said, 'No, he'll be King Edward, like his grandfather.'

And then they'd driven to London, Mummie and Papa, and left behind Lilibet and Margaret Rose with Crawfie at Royal Lodge.

'Don't let all this depress them more than is absolutely necessary, Crawfie: they are so young' – Mummie's words before she left.

Margaret scarcely knew what was going on, as Crawfie spread out their toys on the nursery floor. In the background, the wireless crackled with music. About every half hour it played the 'Dead March' from *Saul* and Allah would burst into tears.

Lilibet had some of her toy horses-on-wheels. With her brush, she tidied their manes, and groomed them as well as she could, but when the 'Dead March' played again, she looked up and said, 'Oh, Crawfie . . . ought we to play?'

'Noughts and crosses!' shrieked Margaret.

So they had an hour of noughts and crosses.

The next day, they were driven up to London. They heard Mummie and Crawfie, in one of their huddles, discussing something. Crawfie was saying, 'I just feel she is too young,' and Mummie whispered something back. Lilibet realized they were discussing whether she should go to Westminster Hall to see the lying-in-state.

It was the first time in her life that Lilibet felt what it meant to be the King of England. King of all these people. As the car drew up outside Westminster Hall, she could see the long line of people, thousands of them, shuffling forward in absolute silence through the ice-cold January day. These were the people of England, many of them in dark, or black, coats, or with black armbands round their ordinary clothes. Lilibet had never seen such a huge crowd. And all still shocked. As if something infinitely precious had been taken from them, and all they could do was shuffle along in silence and bow to the infinite weight of sorrow. There was such dignity in the scene.

Herself wearing a black coat and a little black hat, she climbed out of the car and was led into the Hall. The coffin, draped in the Royal Standard, was placed on a high catafalque, and at each corner stood four men in uniform. But they were not the ordinary Guardsmen. They were Grandpa England's four sons – Papa, Uncle David, Uncle Harry and Uncle Edward. She looked intently at Uncle David, but he did not meet her gaze. He was looking at the ground. He was as still as a statue. His eyelids never flickered. Everything was still. It was as if the old man was asleep and they were afraid to wake him. But it was also as if something had been lost which no one would ever get back.

*   *   *

Then, after the funeral, everything turned rather horribilis. There were many moments, at luncheon or tea, when Papa started to speak, and Mummie gave him one of her looks.

'Bertie, not in front of the children.'

They spoke of 'Her' and 'She' and 'That Woman'.

Grannie, all in black, and with her little black veil over her black toque, said one day, 'She's been staying at the Fort.'

'Huh-huh-huh-*who* has?' Papa had tried to say.

But they all knew, of course. That Woman. Her. The Fort was Fort Belvedere where Uncle David lived, not far from them in Windsor Great Park.

Margaret did not seem to notice these observations and muttered remarks, which spread over the summer months.

They saw much less of Uncle David, even when they were all, the four of them, at Royal Lodge, and Uncle was still staying at the Fort. He had not moved into the Castle as they expected. That Woman again.

'N-n-nothing wrong with having p-p-p—'

Poor Papa could not get out the word 'parties'.

And Mummie had said, 'We're still in mourning! Apart from lack of respect, it's such a lack of good manners. And such parties. You know what I mean.'

Dear, innocent Papa! He looked so baffled when this was said. When she thought about it in grown-up life, Lilibet realized he did not know what sort of parties. He never had raffish friends, and his idea of fun was playing Racing Demon with his daughters, or fishing, or doing a bit of rough shooting at Sandringham or in Windsor Great Park.

Oh, the games of Racing Demon they played that summer and autumn! And then there was that awful day when Mummie came into the nursery, where Papa and the girls were playing with Crawfie, and said, 'He's coming to luncheon.'

'We . . . kn . . . knew that.'

'He's bringing . . .'

'You can't be ssss . . .'

The cards were put away. They all stood at the front door, as Uncle David pulled up in his car. It was one of those moments when you realized how clever Mummie was. She stage-managed it so brilliantly, and it was all so natural-seeming. Uncle David came forward and kissed his nieces as usual, and lifted Margaret Rose in the air, which made her shriek with laughter. And then, as soon

Turning back, Lilibet could see the thin lady who had got out of Uncle David's car.

as her little Start-Rites hit the gravel again, Crawfie said, 'We're going to play in the garden,' and led them off.

Turning back, Lilibet could see the thin lady who had got out of Uncle David's car. Lilibet immediately thought, 'Olive Oyl.' When they did not have Mickey Mouse films, they sometimes watched Popeye the Sailor Man and he had a thin girlfriend, with black hair cut in a tight bob round her head. That was who the lady reminded her of.

They had their luncheon in the schoolroom that day, and it was only at four o'clock, when Uncle David and his friend had left, that the little girls joined Mummie and Papa for tea. Papa hardly ate anything and smoked cigarette after cigarette.

Later – some days or perhaps weeks later – Lilibet heard Mummie saying, 'Not marry her? He must be going mad!'

* * *

That miserable winter day, as the horrible year was coming to an end, they were all back at dear 145. Papa was in the hall, wearing the uniform of an admiral of the Fleet. There had been explosion after explosion with the equerries, the footmen. When he blew up, Mummie stroked his arm and looked compassionately at the latest victim. He couldn't help blowing his top, poor Papa. Anything set him off – a smudge on a footman's button; a pair of shoes insufficiently burnished. Some poor admiral – a real b-b-bounder, Papa said – had come wearing his sword on the wrong side. 'Where do they f-f-f-find these people?'

The house was thick with cigarette smoke.

'You've got to remember,' Mummie said, 'that Uncle David has decided he doesn't want to be the King.'

These words were so shocking that Lilibet had not questioned them.

Every day, she had prayed for Uncle David. 'So replenish him with the grace of thy Holy Spirit, that he may always incline to thy will and walk in thy way . . .'

But he hadn't walked in that Way, had he? It must be because he can never have felt 'it' – what she and Grandpa England had felt on Bognor Beach. He'd never felt that it was the will of God that he should be the King.

'So, because Uncle David has gone abroad – with – with his friend – it means that Papa . . .'

Mummie did not need to finish the sentence, and she did not need to tell their elder daughter what to do when Papa returned to 145 Piccadilly in his admiral's uniform.

Rather than running up to him and kissing him, she walked, in a stately way, towards him and fell into a curtsey. Poor, poor Papa was now the King.

6: Coronation

England, arise! The long, long night is over,
Faint in the East behold the dawn appear,
Out of your evil dream of toil and sorrow –
Arise, O England, for the day is here!
From your fields and hills,
Hark! The answer swells –
Arise, O England, for the day is here!

CRAWFIE USED TO SING IT in her Scottish lilt, walking through Green Park with the dogs and Lilibet and Margaret Rose when they were, in her phrase, knee-high to a grasshopper. Once, at bath-time, Margaret had begun to sing it and Allah had said, 'Now, whoever taught you that?'

'Is there something wrong, Allah?' Lilibet had asked.

'She wouldn't sing it if she remembered . . .' Allah shuddered. 'The very week you were born, Lilibet, the Reds were out on strike. They'd have . . . they'd have . . .'

'What would they have done, Allah?'

'You don't want to know. Only think of what the Russkies did to the poor Tsar. Your cousins. The little children! It makes you shudder to remember. They wouldn't have sung "God Save the King" and that's for sure.'

When they were in their pyjamas, Lilibet had warned her little sister, 'Better not sing "England Arise" any more, Margaret. Especially not in front of Mummie.'

'Who *are* the Reds?'

'Awful stinkers, Mummie says.' Then she had sighed, and added honestly, 'But to tell the truth, I'm not sure that anyone is a stinker when you get to know them properly.'

Why, then, did the song keep coming into her head on the morning of Papa's Coronation? It did not seem like the sort of thing a stinker would sing. Perhaps because, after Uncle David had behaved like an *absolute* stinker and given up the throne, upsetting everyone, especially Grannie England, and marrying That Woman, things had begun to calm down. The long, long night was over. And England was going to arise.

Something had happened to poor Papa. Lilibet knew what it was, and she suspected that no one else, not even

46

Mummie, quite knew what it was. It was the Bognor-on-the-beach thing, the Hand of God had come down on him. He did not need to tell her, but he kept trying to. Even when they were having larks. There'd been that day during the Christmas hols, not long after Papa had become King and they had all moved into BH. They'd all been having a game of Hands, Knees and Boomps-a-Daisy, with Mummie and Crawfie and Allah, and their Lascelles cousins, and Papa had suddenly become grave. And when the game was over and the others were chatting, or offering Margaret a round of Racing Demon, Papa had stood by the window, looking out over the frosty gardens.

'Lilibet, you know what all this . . . means, don't you? For you, I mean.'

'Yes, Papa.'

'It means that, one day, you'll be . . . you'll be . . .'

'Yes, Papa.'

'I have to keep reminding myself,' he had said. 'I sit at my desk, and they bring me documents to sign, and sometimes, I am on the verge of signing with my old name – ALBERT – the way I've always signed, since I learned to write. But I'm not Albert any more. I sign GEORGE R I, and one day . . .'

'Yes, Papa.'

That was why, in the early months of '37, Papa had asked if he could bring Lil to the rehearsals for the Coronation. He spoke so solemnly to her about all the symbolism of it – the crown, the sceptre, the orb – the weight of Majesty.

'The orb is the whole world, our mighty Empire, stretching from shore to shore. The crown shows that I am ... k-k-k ... and the sceptre is the rod of justice, making sure I make life fair for everyone – everyone in the Empire, Lilibet. And we never forget ... never forget why we are here. It is not our crown, or orb or sceptre. We do not own them. They aren't Lilibet's crown or Bertie's orb – the world is God's, the crown is God's, we are His servants, Lilibet.'

And now the day had arrived!

'Rise and shine!' It was Allah's usual way of waking them, and Lilibet had in any case been awake for hours. But Allah's words set off the song inside her head and the stirring tune through all the anxiety of preparation, all the dressing up in their ceremonial robes, all the squabbling with Margaret, who made such silly faces when they pinned her into her velvet and ermine, and through all the majestic Abbey service. England arise, the long, long night is over!

When they were up and dressed, it had been absolutely thrilling. Margaret was only six and she could not stop herself peeping out of the windows. 'Crawfie – look at them!'

And there were the people of England, hundreds, thousands and thousands of them, already lining the Mall, and crowding round the huge white statue of Queen Victoria.

'Do you like my slippers, Crawfie?' Lilibet asked, lifting her long samite dress to reveal silver sandals. They'd been specially made and weren't as comfortable as the Start-Rite ones she had worn for trips to Bognor.

And then they had clambered into the enormous horse-drawn carriages. Allah had brought a bag, because she said the swaying old coach could make you, you know what, but thank heavens *that* did not happen.

'Crawfie, we must make sure that Margaret doesn't wriggle.'

'Don't you mean giggle?' asked the six-year-old little minx.

Because Lilibet had been to the Abbey several times with Papa, for the rehearsals, she had already seen the tiers and banks of seats in the transept, to accommodate all the extra visitors, but she had not been 'backstage'. They were shown into the various canons' rooms. Papa was shown into one of them, accompanied by his valet, armed with packets of Senior Service, and by his Groom of the Robes, Sir Harold Campbell, and Mummie had her Mistress of the Robes. And Allah, armed with hairbrushes and a damp flannel, took the little girls into their room. And in another room, belonging to someone called the Sub-Dean, there was a buffet, laid out with dear little sandwiches, triangles of white bread containing ham and eggs and cheese and cress. There was a nice smell of coffee.

'Crawfie.'

'Yes, my dear?'

'Margaret is too young to come to a coronation. I know she's going to disgrace us. She'll fall asleep or something.'

'You must look after her. You're eleven now and she's still only six.'

There was *one* moment when Lilibet feared disgrace was going to fall on the entire family: Margaret was fiddling with her prayer book and the noise of the large metal clasp sounded to her elder sister's ears like thunder, interrupting the lesson, which was being read so beautifully by one of the bishops.

But the moment passed, and afterwards, she was compelled to admit that her younger sister had behaved very well. You could not expect a child of six to know what was going on. But even a child of eleven who jolly well did know what was going on could not concentrate for the whole of it. And yet . . . even in those moments when her mind was drifting, she was sort of concentrating. She was concentrating on the sad, nervous face of poor darling Papa, as he sat there on the throne of Edward the Confessor. And she thought of Grandpa on the beach, and of all the Kings and Queens of England who had sat there before, holding the orb and sceptre.

And never, ever, would she forget the moment when the Archbishop, Cosmo Gordon Lang, lifted high the crown of St Edward and placed it on poor Papa's head. And all the old peers, in their moth-eaten ermine robes, raised their coronets and shouted out Latin – May he live! May he live! VIVAT! VIVAT!

What a day! As they stood, the four of them, on the balcony of Buckingham Palace, Lilibet thought her numb legs would collapse, she was so tired. The crowds, who cheered and cheered, stretched all the way down the Mall, as far back as Admiralty Arch.

Lilibet had seen the newsreels of the crowds in Italy and Germany, saluting and Heiling and yelling as their dictators in uniform bawled at them through microphones. This was so utterly different. She could not say why. She could never, exactly, say why. But she felt that Papa, in his goodness and decency, and Mummie with her smile, and the crowds, who were, surely, nearly all of them decent,

What a day! As they stood, the four of them, on the balcony of Buckingham Palace, Lilibet thought her numb legs would collapse, she was so tired.

good people who wanted to do their best, were, in some
strange way, 'in it together'?

> *From your fields and hills,*
> *Hark! The answer swells –*
> *Arise, O England, for the day is here!*

7: Buckingham Palace

I T WAS FUNNY, THE STORIES that got themselves repeated in all the 'royal' books and newspaper articles, some of them such absolute rot. One of these was that she felt a prisoner in Buckingham Palace, didn't like the place. Since becoming Queen, she had always loved her apartment there, the corridor, lined with paintings of all the weddings of Queen Victoria's children, and the cosy room with its sofa and its electric fire and the dear old telly, and some favourite pictures on the walls. The Madonna and Child which Sir Anthony Blunt said was probably a Raphael, and that truly wonderful pastel portrait of Jane, her first corgi, which caught her bright eyes so exactly. And the desk. And the photographs of beloved old favourites and best friends – Betsy, in some ways the nicest horse she ever owned, and Burmese, whom she rode eighteen years running for Trooping the Colour, and Sanction, a real friend, whom she had buried at Home Park when he died aged twenty-four. A terrible loss.

And then there were all the racehorses! Aureole, good old Aureole, coming second in the Derby, and Highclere who won the 1,000 Guineas and the Prix de Diane. Phantom Gold, a wonderful horse who'd won the Ribblesdale Stakes at Royal Ascot. And, more recently, of course, Estimate, who'd won the Gold Cup at Royal Ascot and the Doncaster Cup. It was such a comfort to see them all, as she sat at her desk with the red boxes, and it took one's mind off the sadder aspects of life, such as – sometimes, it had to be admitted – the family.

So, she had never regarded Buckingham Palace as a 'prison', and the garden had never ceased to delight her, this huge expanse of lawns and shrubberies, and glorious herbaceous borders, acre upon acre of it in the middle of London. From their first day in BP, Lilibet and Margaret Rose had made friends with the ducks. And the summer house where dear old Grandpa England had liked to sit, doing his boxes. (They had left his writing table and pens and pencils just as they had been.)

The children ate their meals in the nursery. There was a nursery footman now! He would carry the food upstairs.

Yes, things were much more formal in the Palace, but they were only there for a few months each year, and many a week they all retreated to Royal Lodge in Windsor, where life was still its happy, intimate self, or to Balmoral, which they all loved, especially if there were young officers from one of the Scottish regiments staying. Always ready for a game of sardines or musical chairs after dinner. Or to Sandringham, which Papa loved because of the shooting.

The worst wrench, for Lilibet and Margaret Rose, was in 1939, when the King and Queen did a tour of Canada and the United States. Only when they had gone, did Lilibet realize how much she cherished Mummie and the warm, happy, informal atmosphere she created around them. Once, the King rang up from Canada, and Lilibet held up Dookie to the receiver so that she could bark to her master down the phone. Poor Dookie – Lord Lothian, who was the lord-in-waiting who took the call, did not know how to handle a dog, so no wonder Dookie gave him a little nip. Well, quite a big nip actually – there was blood all over the carpet.

Of course, the other members of the family did their very best to make the girls happy. Queen Mary told Crawfie to take the time off, and she herself supervised endless visits to museums and galleries, which enthralled Margaret, but which Lilibet, if she was truthful, found rather a bore. One old relic in a glass case, be it precious china or jewellery or a painting, was much like another, as far as Lilibet was concerned, and she had always preferred animals and the outdoors.

David and Michael Bowes-Lyon – Mummie's brothers – took the girls off for weekends, but it wasn't the same as when We Four were all together. A huge relief when they were taken by Crawfie down to Southampton to meet the *Empress of Britain*, sailing into the Solent. Mummie had exclaimed that both the girls had lost weight, and Margaret had said, 'At least I don't look like a football any more.'

Of course, by then, the news was awful. Day after day. The wireless, which had so often been a source of merriment for all of them, now made one's flesh creep, with Germany taking back Austria, and wanting the Rhineland back from the French, which really would, Mummie said, put the cat among the p. And Churchill, who had annoyed them all so much championing Uncle David and That Woman, now seeming positively to *want* a war. Surely, Papa said, Lord Halifax was right and one should try to sort everything out by talking sensibly, like gentlemen.

'Papa,' Margaret had asked one day at tea at Royal Lodge. 'Who *is* this Hitler, spoiling everything?'

Mummie said she had heard that, if you knew German – which of course she did not, nor did she want Lilibet or Margaret to learn it, thanks very much – he sounded completely common. Not that one liked to think in that way. Papa said, if only Lord Halifax were Prime Minister, even though you could see that Mr Chamberlain was doing his best. They believed that the Chamberlains, who had produced such famous politicians in recent generations, had begun in a very humble way, manufacturing. Nothing at all wrong with that, and jolly good luck to them. But Lord Halifax was a dear, and great friends, of course, with the Lascelles family in Yorkshire.

8: Dartmouth

I N THIS HAPPY PHASE OF sleep, she was sniffing the sea
air, as she stood on the deck of the Royal Yacht.

Just before their annual summer departure for
Balmoral, in that last month before the outbreak of war, the
King and Queen had sailed on the Royal Yacht, *Victoria and
Albert*, on a visit to Dartmouth Naval College, where Papa
had trained as a midshipman before the First World War.

They loved sailing on the large, gold and white yacht, a
true survivor of the old days, with its massive figurehead,
rich Victorian fittings and its cabins decorated with
cretonne. Lilibet loved the yacht. She loved her neat little
cabin, which was next to Margaret's. (Mummie and Papa
slept amidships.) She loved being at sea. Papa had been
in the Royal Navy, and he always looked happier when
he was in uniform.

Memory would paint that August, the last month of peace, as a glorious, sunny, happy few weeks. The wind was in the quarter-deck. Every day on the yacht felt like a special holiday. The little girls were allowed to eat in the dining room with their parents, a truly sailor-like experience, since the main mast came out and up through one end of the dining table.

After only a day at sea, they reached the mouth of the River Dart and approached the vast redbrick of the college. The estuary, which glittered with silver sunlight, was crowded with little sailing boats.

The King was to inspect the officers and cadets on their parade ground; then they would file into the chapel for a service of thanksgiving, and the two Princesses would be given the chance to meet the cadets. Margaret and Crawfie had been singing 'Every Nice Girl Loves a Sailor', which, though she considered it highly amusing, Lilibet felt was a little lacking in dignity.

And then came the awful news. A motor-launch pulled up alongside. A young officer came aboard the yacht, and the grown-ups had grouped into a huddle.

It was Mummie who broke the news.

'Girls – you are not to be coming with us—' There was the explanation, interrupted before it was quite finished by Margaret asking, 'What's mumps?'

Without medical explanation, Crawfie told them that they did not want to be catching the mumps just before their summer holiday. There had been several cases in the college and it was considered unwise that the Princesses should come into the chapel and risk infection.

'Very kindly *indeed*,' said Mummie, 'the Dalrymple-Hamiltons have offered to give you both tea, while Papa and I go to the chapel service.'

But who were they? And how could meeting the Dalrymple-Hamiltons be any possible consolation for the pain of missing a visit to the cadets?

The family lived in the Captain's House at the college, and there were two children. They had laid out a clockwork railway on the nursery floor. Lilibet was thirteen years old! Far too old for a toy railway. But with her usual politeness, she knelt down and pretended to be interested. Margaret chattered merrily to the children, who were a little older than they were. And then the nursery door opened.

A young cadet in uniform brought in a tray of lemonade and ginger biscuits. He was followed by a slightly older cadet: a blond-haired youth, with a sharp, clever face and piercing blue eyes.

'Are you going to eat all those ginger nuts yourselves or does a chap stand any chance of having one?' he barked.

Somehow, you knew the mischief was all a joke, and Lilibet began to laugh. Her eyes met those bright blue eyes of the Viking.

'We've never met,' he told her. 'My name's Philip Mountbatten.'

When the plate of ginger nuts had been gobbled, he said, 'Let's go down to the tennis courts.'

'I'm not sure where the rackets . . .' began one of the Dalrymple-Hamilton children. But Philip had replied, 'Who said anything about rackets?' and was making them laugh by pretending that the net in the centre of the court was a hurdle. He leapt over it.

'Oh, Crawfie!' said Lilibet. 'Look how high he can jump!'

She would have done anything to persuade Mummie to allow her to stay up that evening. There was to be a dinner and dancing. But it was decreed that 'the children' must have an early supper and go to bed. As she lay in her bunk on the Royal Yacht, Lilibet could hear the music of the Palais Glide and the Lambeth Walk drifting across the water.

He came for lunch on the yacht the next day, and they spent the day together.

'You must stay for tea,' said the Queen. 'It will be your last meal of the day.'

'We've never met,' he told her. 'My name's Philip Mountbatten.'

He was Prince Philip of Greece. He was a cousin. A fairly distant one. He was the most beautiful being Lilibet had ever seen.

He smilingly accepted, as Lilibet brought him plateful after plateful of shrimps. And then –

'Have a banana split!'

'Are you trying to give me a pot belly?'

The happiness which had come upon her . . . it was strange. She had been happy, surely, always? How could she not have been happy, with Mummie, and Papa and Crawfie and Bobo and Margaret? But this . . . this was a new sort of happiness. Her heart was dancing. And the time did not merely go fast, it whizzed.

Before she had accustomed herself to the swooping sensation of joy – and could she *ever* accustom herself to this, since it was ecstasy, it was bliss, it was even more enjoyable than riding a pony – he was being ushered out of the cabin, onto the deck, he was bowing to the King and Queen and half running down the gangplank.

As the *Victoria and Albert* pulled away, down the Dart and out to sea, the boys of Dartmouth commandeered any small boat they could find to escort the royal party. It was a wonderful flotilla, but as they approached the river mouth, the captain in charge, Sir Dudley North, gave the order that they should turn back. It was no longer safe and they were entering the choppy waters of the Channel.

All the cadets obeyed, all except one. One little rowing boat continued to follow the Royal Yacht.

'Please, Papa! May I?'

Lilibet took her father's binoculars and was able to see the Viking, pulling with his strong arms, as his little craft rose higher and swooped lower in the mounting waves.

'The young . . . f-f—f-f-f-' The King was having one of his outbursts of rage, and the word 'fool' was difficult to stammer out. 'He must go back, or we shall have to heave to and send him back!'

The captain was bawling through a megaphone at the young scamp.

Lilibet could see through the binos that Philip was laughing. There was that mischievous laugh, as he put down one of the oars on the floor of the boat and waved vigorously.

She suddenly thought, 'I am on board the *Victoria and Albert*, those two royal cousins who fell in love a hundred years ago, and that is why we are here – me, and Papa and . . . and . . . *him* . . .'

'The f-f-f—fool! M-mm-mmake him go b-b-back!'

Did anyone see her? She had allowed the binoculars to drop onto her chest. She had raised her hand and was waving enthusiastically. As the great Victorian yacht glided out to sea, she still waved, until they left the rowing boat behind, and the blond figure who sat in it became a tiny distant speck.

9: Jane

'HOW DID THE DOG GET in here?'

The answer was not audible.

The Queen was not quite asleep. She was in that state between sleep and waking, between consciousness and a greater dark. She did not speak. She was not sure that she could speak. She could hear the voices, and feel the fuss, and quietly, deeply, hoped it would go away, leaving her alone with . . . Her hands were outside the bedding. One hand touched a damp nose, and the other hand clasped the fur. She was not sure whether the voices were speaking now – whether the footman had come in with the morning tea – or whether it was just memory again, sighing through her mind, half waking and half sleeping, as earth rolled onward into night.

'Jane?'

67

The voices were fussing. Who had allowed the dog in? Who could lift it off the bed without awaking or disturbing the old lady who lay there? With one hand, she stroked, and with the other she held the fur, as tightly as she could.

'Leave it. Leave the dog. She's stroking him.'

'Do you think she even knows if he is there?'

Sleep . . . Or something like sleep. There was no time any more, but she could feel the moist nose and the reddish foxy fur of Jane. They were out in the Great Park. Jane had been chasing rabbits. In the air, a solitary Spitfire was passing overhead.

The summer of '40, was it? When Mummie had told them they must leave Royal Lodge and move into the Castle? They had left in a hurry for their new lives, of gas masks and air raids and austere meals. They carried the tiny suitcases themselves, with only enough clothes for a weekend, never guessing that they would live in the Lancaster Tower for the next five years.

Jane had come with them. How could they ever be parted from Jane, Lil's favourite corgi? Dookie, who had been Mummie and Papa's favourite, had died at the very beginning of the war, so now Jane was top dog. She brought her two pups with her, who had been born at Sandringham one Christmas Day and had the inevitable names of Crackers and Carol.

Dear Jane! In those lonely, early months, when they were isolated at Windsor without Mummie and Papa (who stayed behind in London), Jane was her best friend. Her old hands felt for her now in the mysterious darkness.

That terrible day, when she was out with Jane in the park. The foxy little dog was chasing a rabbit.

'There's one, Jane!'

Margaret, Crawfie and Lilibet stood on the grass verge, watching the white tail of the bunny chasing across the grass, onto the tarmac and into the thick grass on the other side of the road.

Jane let out barks of pure joy and, on her short legs, she ran out into the road.

It all happened so quickly. A gardener, driving his dark green van, had appeared, seemingly from nowhere. The van swerved. The man jammed on the brakes, but it was too late.

He scrunched to a halt, opened the van door, ran round.

Lilibet felt two overwhelming and very different sorts of pain, as, clutching the poor little dead body of Jane, she looked up into the troubled face of the gardener. She felt a grief too deep to be expressed. And for the man. She felt so, so sorry.

* * *

They must have driven her back to the Castle. She could not remember. The moment which survived was the moment of holding the dog. She was still warm. And that sad, frightened face of the man.

Dear Jane. Dear, dear Jane. Of course, there were Crackers and Carol, who went on being her friends for years after that. Much, much later, for her eighteenth birthday, the King gave her Susan, the first corgi who was exclusively her own. Susan's kennel name had been Hickathrift Pippa, but Lilibet had immediately renamed her Susan. She had been a red and white, like Dookie and Jane, and lived long into the lifetime of the children, who of course never really saw the point of Susan. Well, children don't always.

The staff always said that Susan was a snarler, but to Lilibet she had never been anything other than a charmer. Yes, she once bit one of the Guards outside Buckingham Palace, but that was years after the war. She had also bitten the royal clock winder – was he called Mr Hubbard?

Poor Hubbard, but if you know how to handle a dog it will not bite! She remembered an incident when the children had been young. Charles and Anne had been out for a walk in St James's Park, when Honey – nice little Honey – had sunk her teeth into a young Irish Guardsman's bottom. But the children did not know how to deal with Honey, that was the reason for that.

All the corgis of a lifetime were with her . . . Dookie, Jane, Crackers, Carol, Susan, Honey, Heather, Tinker, Brush, Buzz, Foxy, Sugar, Shadow, Smokey, Clipper, Sparky, Whisky, Myth, Fable, Jolly, Socks, Piper, Tiny.

Dogs were easier than children. As she lay there in the darkness of her mind, her hands stroked, and the wet nose nuzzled, and it was as if, like a multitude of the heavenly host, all the corgis of a lifetime were with her . . . Dookie, Jane, Crackers, Carol, Susan, Honey, Heather, Tinker, Brush, Buzz, Foxy, Sugar, Shadow, Smokey, Clipper, Sparky, Whisky, Myth, Fable, Jolly, Socks, Piper, Tiny. Each one of them had possessed such a distinct personality. They seemed, all of them, to be with her. With her always.

* * *

As soon as they returned to the Lancaster Tower, after the accident, she had asked Crawfie for writing paper and an envelope. She could not get the sad gardener's face out of her mind. In her neat, firm handwriting, she wrote him a letter; said that she realized it was not his fault, he could not possibly have seen Jane as she ran out in front of the van, begged him not to blame himself . . .

'You will make sure he gets the letter, Crawfie? This afternoon. Do send it to him, directly, won't you?'

* * *

Windsor. Always Windsor, during those wartime years. They had been there for Christmas 1940, when she had given her first broadcast to the children of Great Britain. So many rehearsals! So many rewritings of the words, at the behest of Mummie! And then, on the day, she had asked Margaret to come to the microphone. 'Come, Margaret, say good night! Good night, children.'

It must have been funny for members of the Household to hear one's voice coming out of the wireless. So much of wartime experience came to them filtered through that large wooden contraption, with its gigantic speaker. It needed to be warmed up, and during this process, it sometimes squeaked or growled, as if it were alive and trying to clear its throat. Then it would be *ITMA* – wonderfully funny, Tommy Handley, speaking from the Ministry of Aggravation and Mysteries or the Office of Twerps, or sometimes from the seaside town of Foaming-at-the-Mouth. How utterly horrible it was when Lord Haw-Haw came on – *Chairmany calling! Chairmany calling!* That silky, cruel voice. How eagerly they always tuned into the news, and how terrifying the news so often was – Denmark, Norway, Holland, Belgium, France, all falling to the invasion of the Nazis. Through the wireless had come all the news of disasters – Dunkirk, the Fall of Singapore, the sinking of the *Ark Royal* – as well as, of course, eventually, the triumphs – El Alamein, the Allied landings in Italy, D Day and, a year or so later, Victory. One lived through the wireless, and had done really ever since, though Radio 2 wasn't the same since the death of dear Jimmy Young.

* * *

It was at Windsor, oh so slowly, that the reality had dawned. Since Papa became King, she had known, of course she had known, that one day she would wear the crown. But it was not possible to absorb the knowledge, to make it real. She remembered one day, it was raining so hard outside that they found nothing to do. She always hated a day when she could not be out walking the dogs, or riding one of her ponies. Sitting in their schoolroom, utterly bored, swinging their legs against their desks, they had looked up and seen the King's Librarian, Sir Owen Morshead.

'Would you like to see something interesting?'

They followed eagerly.

However many times you explored the spiral staircases and wandered down stone-flagged corridors and passageways, you felt lost.

Margaret was saying, with heavy sarcasm, 'I'm sure it is going to be *really* interesting!' as they followed Sir Owen down the warren, down, down, round the bend, up a few

74

steps, down, down, down again. They were in the vaults, now, deep beneath the earth. Sir Owen shone a pocket torch on a row of pillowcases and blankets on a shelf.

'I told you it would be interesting,' Margaret said.

The man reached out for one of them. He unwrapped from the blanket what appeared to be an ordinary leather hat-box.

'Open it,' he said.

When Margaret reached out her hand, he said, 'Perhaps Princess Elizabeth.'

'Why should *she* be the one who opens it first?'

Crawfie, behind her, said simply, 'Margaret.'

Lilibet's fingers reached for the clasp of the leather case and opened it. She had no idea what she was going to find. There was a hard, bejewelled cross, and beneath it, a golden arch, clustering around velvet. In the torchlight, jewels winked.

'Is it?' she asked.

She could see Sir Owen Morshead smiling. 'You remember the Coronation, don't you . . .'

She remembered the Archbishop placing this crown on Papa's head. There it was!

'We decided it was not safe to leave the Crown Jewels in the Tower of London while the bombs were falling, and who knows . . .'

'Do you think the Germans might come into London?' she asked.

'Never,' said the man loyally. 'But the jewels will be safer here. Only two or three of us know where they are. The King, myself . . .'

'And now us!' said Lilibet.

Of course, it was perfectly killing, because, rather later in the war, Sir Owen told Papa, with a pale face and a shaking voice, that he had forgotten where he'd hidden them, and for about a week it was Hunt the Thimble.

'Rather a big thimble,' Papa had said.

But she never forgot it. As they watched the Royal Librarian replace the Crown Jewels in their leather case, and wrap them again in their blankets and put them back on the shelf, Lil had been visited by a strange foreboding.

most difficult with their mothers, and of course Mummie was staying behind in London to look the East End in the face and to stand by Papa's side. So all those 'teenage' tensions, which one could remember so well when Anne was that age, were avoided. Some families avoid them by sending the teenagers to a boarding school. But in the Firm, when she and Margaret were young, they had done it simply by separation.

Sometimes Mummie and Papa came to Windsor, of course they did. One remembered the evening when Mummie suddenly decided that the Little Princesses did not have enough literature in their lives, and Mummie's friends the Sitwells organized a Poetry Evening. Osbert and Edith had read some of their beautiful verses and then this lugubrious chap who looked like a bank manager in a pinstripe suit sort of chanted to them this poem he had written called *The Waste Land*. The one thing one mustn't do is giggle. Lilibet had known that from an early age. But it was like when you get the giggles in church, it somehow wouldn't die down. The girls saw that Papa's shoulders were shaking, and then Mummie started to laugh, and so finally, Lilibet and Margaret simply *burst*. Poor man. He was probably extremely famous and everything, but really one could not stop oneself, and as for what he was saying, or chanting, well, it really was incomprehensible.

*   *   *

Otherwise, the Princesses were left rather to themselves. There was Alathea, a tall, rather awkward girl, two years older than Lilibet herself. She was spending the war with her grandfather, Lord Fitzalan, at Cumberland Lodge. Lord Fitzalan had been the last Viceroy of Ireland. A left-footer, Mummie said, but many of them were perfectly sweet, though one couldn't beat the dear old C of E. Bobo – their old nurserymaid who never left Lilibet's side – used to say, 'If Alathea had been a boy, she'd have been a Duke. And not just any Duke. Duke of Norfolk, who organizes the Coronations.'

But she wasn't a boy, and although she was older than Lilibet, she always seemed a bit childish. They had dancing lessons with her, and drawing lessons, and endless games: charades, blind man's buff, clumps, the whispering game and cards, cards, cards: Old Maid or Racing Demon.

With Alathea, and some of the other girls whose parents worked on the estate or in the Household, and with the evacuee children who had come out of the East End to escape the bombing, they had formed a Guide troop. They were all determined to get their cookery badge.

That was when she made a discovery about herself which had always made her a little uncomfortable. They used to prepare stews, which they then gave to the ARP wardens on duty in the Castle.

'Lilibet is so clever,' Crawfie used to say. 'She can slice onions without it making her cry.'

It was true, but it wasn't clever. The strange fact was, she did not cry. Though it seemed profane to admit it, even to herself, in her most private thoughts, she was always troubled by the Christmas hymn 'Away in a Manger' – 'The Little Lord Jesus no crying he makes'. Lilibet did not cry. Margaret Rose used to weep buckets – when she did not get her own way, when Allah made her wear a blue woollen cardie rather than a green one, and, of course, during films. But tears almost never came to Lilibet's eyes. The only times she had felt her eyes moistening in her entire life were when they buried Sanction, and when she left the Royal Yacht *Britannia* for the last time. She asked herself sometimes, was it just a physical thing, or – rather frightening, the alternative – was she a teeny bit heartless?

But – the Guides! Most of the time, they were not slicing vegetables, they were making scones, or cakes.

One rather foolish convention had developed. There were plenty of eggs on the home farms in Windsor, but they kept strictly to the rule of eating only one egg per week, for their breakfast on Sundays, as if they had to buy rationed eggs. Illogically, however, they did make cakes in the Guides' cooking classes, using tons of eggs, and all the children used to eat these. Only, when the King and Queen came to tea with the Guides, they just ate bread and butter. Mummie said they *must* stick to rations, like everyone else in the country, who were going through so much.

* * *

Crawfie tried to join the Women's Royal Naval Service, the Wrens, but the Queen was against it. 'You'd only be cooking some old admiral his breakfast,' was what Mummie said, and she was probably right. Said that Crawfie's patriotic duty was to stay in Windsor with the Little Princesses.

But the Little Princesses were not so little as the years passed. As she grew up, it became clear that Lilibet would want to 'do her bit' like others of her age. Mummie and Papa were against it. She insisted, however, and joined the Auxiliary Territorial Service. Wearing her Guides uniform, she registered when she was sixteen, at the Labour Exchange in Windsor. She was Number 230873 Second Subaltern Elizabeth Alexandra Mary Windsor. It was the only time in her entire life when she could truly test her own capabilities against others of her own age.

'The Princess is to be treated in exactly the same way as any other officer learning at the driving training centre.' That was what the official report said, at the very outset. She learned to drive and to do basic motor maintenance. She kept to the routine of the ATS mess. She undertook simple duties, like all the other young women. Every evening, though, she returned to the Castle to sleep. She was living in two worlds, and it took a year for her to pass all her tests. Every morning, it was her duty to drive the commandant over to the ATS depot at Camberley. She also drove the Red Cross van, which made Margaret, still stuck in the schoolroom, explode with envy. She drove during air raids. She negotiated her van round London in the blackout. That had been an adventure!

*　*　*

It was during the pantomimes that she became fully aware that she was no longer a child. It was not the first year. It was the time when Papa, who took a great interest in the

She drove during air raids. She negotiated her van round London in the blackout.

last-minute rehearsals and arrangements, looked at her in her Aladdin outfit and said, 'She can't possibly wear that: the tunic is much too short.' She realized then that she had enjoyed the looks she'd been getting from the young Guards officers and the visiting American officers.

When the Christmas plays began, such intimations were unknown, or anyway unrecognized. The first one they did was something they had planned to put on at Birkhall or Balmoral, the first Christmas of the war, in case they were stuck up there. (Luckily, they'd come south in the end.) It was called *The Christmas Child*, and Lilibet took the part of one of the Wise Men. She wore a golden crown and a velvet tunic made out of an old curtain. The child in the shepherd's hut, who sang 'Gentle Jesus, Meek and Mild', was Margaret, aged eight. The play was well rehearsed, with evacuee children as fellow cast members, and the performance took place in St George's Hall.

Next year, the master of the school in Windsor Great Park, Mr Tanner, wrote a panto for his pupils. Margaret was given the role of Cinderella and Lilibet was the Principal Boy, Prince Florizel. Mr Tanner cast poor Alathea as Agatha Blimp, a name which, one was very much afraid, rather stuck. The jokes were nearly all puns.

Margaret: We've got a large copper in the kitchen.

Lilibet: We'll soon get rid of him.

Which brought the house down. Next year, when they did *Sleeping Beauty*, Lilibet had put her arms through the arms of two young sailors and sung 'Mind Your Sisters'. The audience thumped their feet on the floor, clapped and roared.

Four hundred people came to hear her Aladdin. They raised a lot of money for Mummie's Wool Fund – it was to knit mufflers, mittens and so forth for the troops. And in the last panto, Lilibet played a Victorian seaside belle. She was aware of herself blushing when she asked, 'Who do you think is coming to see us act, Crawfie?'

It was Philip, of course, now a young man. He had fought a gallant war in the Navy, been mentioned in dispatches after the battles of Crete and Matapan, and was now, as Lieutenant, Second-in-Command of HMS *Wallace*. There was something serious, chiselled and sad about him at first, but once the show started, and she could see him in the front row of the Waterloo Room, she could see his sharp merry eyes focused upon her, and she could hear him laughing, cheering and shouting, 'Encore!'

11: VE Day

AY 1945: VERY NEARLY EIGHT years since Papa's Coronation on 12 May 1937. The world had turned upside down. Uncle David had not been heard of – certainly not spoken of – for years. Uncle Edward was dead. So many, many people were dead! And for the whole conflict, they had been in Windsor, and when they left it, she and Margaret Rose, they would leave behind their innocent childhoods.

While they were dressing that Sunday at Royal Lodge, 6 May, and getting ready for church, the phone went. At any moment, the war in Europe was going to be over. Margaret and Lilibet piled into the car with Mummie and Papa and roared back to London. On 8 May, when Victory in Europe Day began, the Palace was surrounded by surging crowds, roaring and shouting and cheering.

When they had watched the terrible newsreels all through the war, they had become so used to unhappy crowds – to the frenzied, hypnotized Germans, Heil Hitlering. As Mummie used to say, one would feel an absolute Charlie addressing a British politician in that way – Hail Joynson-Hicks, for example. And just as bad, one thought of all the countless tiers of Soviet troops, like automata, paraded before 'Uncle Joe'. ('No Uncle of mine,' Papa used to say. 'He *murdered* my cousins.') And, more lately, they had seen the burning cities, the refugees in their hundreds and thousands streaming from ruins, and pouring down roads where every tree was scorched to charcoal and every church was a smoking wreck.

And having seen so many horrible such spectacles on their newsreel screens in the cinema at Windsor Castle, they were now in the capital, and they could hear the voices soaring up from the Mall – 'WE WANT THE KING! WE WANT THE KING!'

It went on all through the day. Eventually, Mummie told the King that they *must* go out on the balcony, with Lilibet and Margaret. When they did so, the noise was like a huge ocean roar. Later in the day, Mr Churchill had come to lunch at the Palace, and afterwards, he had gone out onto the balcony with them and given his famous

And then Margaret had said, 'I think we should go out in the crowd.'

V for Victory sign. More roars. And then Margaret had said, 'I think we should go out in the crowd.'

Lilibet had thought her sister had gone mad, but Papa had surprised her by saying, 'You know, you are right. What do you think, Tommy?'

And Sir Alan Lascelles, the King's Private Secretary – Tommy – had said, 'So long as they have a guard . . .'

So, it was arranged. A police sergeant would go with them, and a small party of their Grenadier Guards friends. They slipped out of the side gate in Buckingham Palace Road and walked down to Parliament Square. Then they went to their old childhood stamping ground in Piccadilly, down St James's Street, Bennet Street, across Berkeley Square and Park Lane. They had gone into the Dorchester – the only place where Lilibet thought they had (perhaps) been recognized. It was difficult to know, because everyone was greeting everyone else. There was the most extraordinary sense of collective happiness, euphoria, relief. Total strangers embraced, or at the very least greeted one another as friends. They did not appear to be drunk. There wasn't enough drink for any but the very lucky to have overindulged.

Eventually, they had come across Green Park, and they pressed through the crowds to the railings of the Palace and joined in the chanting, WE WANT THE KING! WE

WANT THE KING! And there was Papa on the balcony again. There was a connection between the King and the crowds. There could never be a connection like that between a politician and a crowd, however clever the politician had been at wowing them with speeches through microphones. This was something quite different. It was like knowing your family. It was a real bond, not just a feeling of admiration or attraction. It was *it*. It was what one had always known, since Bognor.

WE WANT THE KING! WE WANT THE KING!

12: Married

THERE WAS A STIRRING, SOMEWHERE in the darkened room. One never woke, after the fire, without thinking it was going to happen all over again. That terrible feeling, not only that Windsor Castle was going up in flames, but that everything they had all worked so hard to maintain, ever since she was born in 1926, was being destroyed – stability, religion, kindliness, a feeling of goodwill towards one another.

Were there really people, coming and going, in her bedroom, or were they, rather, drifting in and out of her dreams? The 'Annus Horribilis'. The awful newspaper stories, involving her children. The rumours. The tittle-tattle. The films about her and her family. The satires, as they were termed.

People were so cruel. They said that, now, the Royal Family all looked like hypocrites, sending Uncle David into exile, and refusing to acknowledge That Woman. Well, marriage was a long journey and it was not always an easy one, as she and Philip would have been the first to acknowledge.

When was it – not long after her own marriage – she had made that speech to the Mothers' Union, and the papers got so hot and bothered? Even then.

'We can have no doubt that divorce and separation are responsible for some of the darkest evils in our society today . . . I believe there is a great fear in our generation of being labelled priggish . . .'

When the protests hit the headlines, Mummie and Papa supported her. 'Their views on marriage and family life were the same.'

'Mummy' . . . 'Mummy' . . . Who was talking to her now? One of the children? She reached out, and could only feel the little dog who lay beside her on the bed-covering.

Children? Or dream-children? Poor children. It had been harder for them than for her. Uncle David had been right. Papa and Mummie had a blessing which had been denied to him – a happy home, with one another, and their children. We Four.

It had been such a very happy day, the wedding day: Lilibet in that stupendous dress by Norman Hartnell, Philip – simply 'Lieutenant Philip Mountbatten R.N.' on the Order of Service – looking breathtakingly handsome. And they had all sung 'Crimond' – Bobo's suggestion – which at that date had been largely unknown in Great Britain and was now one of the most popular of hymns.

> *Yea, though I walk in Death's dark vale,*
> *Yet will I fear none ill . . .*

Coming down the aisle of the Abbey, arm in arm, they had paused as they came past the King, and Lilibet had given a deep curtsey. The dress had billowed out like a cloud around and behind her.

After the wedding breakfast at Buckingham Palace, the King and Queen had joined the other guests, running out into the forecourt throwing rose petals at the pair, Philip still in his uniform, Lilibet by then in her love-in-a-mist blue coat. They sat in an open landau, and a crowd followed them all the way to Waterloo Station, pursued by roll upon roll of cheers. Crackers was with them in the landau.

They spent the honeymoon at Broadlands, Uncle Dickie's house. Uncle was just back from India – the last Viceroy. The Raj and the Empire were over, but the special something – the something she had felt was handed down from George V – continued, and this feeling was increased, in November 1948, when Charles was born. (No Home Secretary present! Tommy Lascelles had put a stop to that nonsense.) The monarchy now had a future.

Just for a while, however, she and Philip had private lives of their own. Philip was appointed First Lieutenant and Second-in-Command of HMS *Chequers*, Leader of the First Destroyer Flotilla of the Mediterranean Fleet. For the next two years, they would be based in Malta, living in Villa Guardamangia, Uncle Dickie's house. When Philip was busy, Lilibet would drive her Daimler round the island, alone, or with a female companion. When he was free, he and the Mountbattens would accompany her on swimming expeditions, or trips on their launch to creeks and bays around the island. From time to time, she would return to England, to conduct official duties, or to watch Monaveen, a horse she owned jointly with Mummie, win at Hurst Park on odds of 10 to 1. Charles was looked after perfectly adequately, much of this time, at Sandringham.

Philip's naval career was a great success. He was promoted to Lieutenant-Commander and given command of the frigate HMS *Magpie*. True, she could not always be in Malta (in 1950, for instance, she came home to give birth to another child, Anne), but memory painted a continuous picture of freedom, of bright sun on the vivid Mediterranean blue, of picnics and laughter, and love.

At the back of their minds, there was always the knowledge that this freedom and this independence could not last. Papa was ill. She would be needed more and more to undertake duties on his behalf. But for a time, a precious, short, wonderful time, they were free.

Only one cloud: and who would ever have guessed it? Crawfie! While they were in Malta, they heard that Crawfie, who, of course, was no longer needed as their governess, had written her memoirs – *The Little Princesses* – and they were going to be serialized in an American magazine.

Until it happened, Lilibet had only been sporadically aware of the 'public' intruding into her private life. She felt deep attachment to all the millions of people in the Empire, of course she did. And a duty to them. And she knew that, for instance, when she and Philip had been courting there had been 'interest' in the newspapers – gossipy articles about him taking her to see *Oklahoma!*, that sort of thing. Funnily enough, it really was true that she loved the song from that show, 'People Will Say

We're in Love', though how the *Daily Express* should have known, she had no idea!

But Crawfie's book was different from gossip in the papers. Crawfie had made her and Margaret, Mummie and Papa into 'characters' in a storybook. They had a different sort of existence now. It was no longer quite possible to believe that their lives were their own. Mummie said it was best not to read Crawfie's book, and that was good advice. But Margaret read it, of course, and said it was absolute drivel – for instance, claiming that Lilibet was not a good sailor and had been sick on their voyage to the Channel Islands. But it was not little details like this which made Crawfie's book such a shock. It was her treachery, and worse than that, even – it was this thing of making them all, all the details of their private life, a spectacle.

When she had been a child, arranging the shoes under her bed or playing with her toy horses, or pretending to cook meals with Margaret in the Little House, that pair of beady eyes had been taking it all in; and rather than simply looking at her with affection, an affection in which both Princesses had always believed, Crawfie had been a spy. When they both started to travel the world, Philip or she were sometimes told of peoples in some remote forest or mountain hideaway who did not want to be photographed, who felt their souls or identities would somehow be stolen from them if they were made into pictures inside a camera. Lilibet so understood that. Crawfie had stolen their inner life, made it into a story, taken their insides out, and in a funny way, they would never go back in.

13: A Woman Alone

SHE COULD HEAR COUGHING, BUT it might not have been anyone here or now. It was probably somewhere in the back of her mind. Cough, cough, cough.

And, as happens in these Night Thoughts which occur between waking and sleeping, two or three sensations blended into one. The hearing – cough, cough. The stab of fear and pity as she heard it. And as she had these feelings of sympathy and fear, she could see her father's ashen, wrinkled face, the face of an old man, though he was a long way short of his sixtieth birthday.

The doctors did everything possible, except to persuade him to give up the cigarettes. During Queen Mary's eighty-fourth birthday party, both Grannie and Papa had smoked like chimneys, but he was not well enough, a few days later, to greet dear King Haakon of Norway who was over on a visit and had been such a hero during the war. Lilibet had presided at the dinner for him – the first really big 'do' she had hosted.

The event, though, which made it clear, not only to her, but to the world, that she was the monarch in waiting had been the Trooping the Colour ceremony for the Brigade of Guards in Whitehall. She had ridden out side-saddle on Burmese. 'A woman alone,' *The Times* had said.

Mummie did what she could, standing in for Papa, but by the autumn of 1950 it was clear that more than bed rest was going to be needed to cure these persistent bouts of what seemed like flu.

That September, when they returned from Balmoral with the children, Charles and Anne, Lilibet and her husband were told the news. The King's advanced cancer would necessitate the removal of his left lung.

The operation happened in Buckingham Palace and there was a huge crowd, waiting silently for the result. Lilibet remembered the hours of waiting, while Papa had been under the anaesthetic. As well as her anguish for a beloved father, she felt an aching sympathy for Philip. His taut, worried features told the whole story. Their life of public duty had begun. Papa was never going to be well enough to undertake many public duties again, and the burden would fall on them.

When he had left Malta, Philip had been told that he must not accept any further naval appointments. He was barely thirty. It had been such a happy time in Malta, just the two of them. The newspapers had attacked them as 'uncaring' parents, for getting the children sent to Sandringham for Christmas while Lilibet and Philip stayed behind on the island – but really, the children were so young, they would not notice their absence – not as her dogs and horses noticed when one went away and really missed one. When it was all over, Philip sadly put away his snorkel and fishing gear and water skis, and said to her, 'I don't suppose I'll be wanting these again.'

And so it had proved. They had gone to Canada and the United States to represent the King. When they arrived at the White House, President Truman introduced her to his mother-in-law, who said, 'Honey, I'm so pleased for you – your father's been re-elected.' There was a jolt on one's heart. What did she mean . . .? But she had only wanted to say that Winston Churchill had won the election for the Conservatives.

President Truman was one of the many men at this stage of her life who fell in love with her. She could feel it. More than a fatherly affection. She noticed so many men falling for her – were they in love with her or with what she was going to become? Such a strange little man, Truman, in his specs and his well-cut lawyer's suit. He looked completely harmless, and yet this was the only person in history who had actually used the atomic bomb – twice.

'Do you suppose the King will be well enough to do the Australia and New Zealand tour next year?' Philip had asked. The question did not need answering. Lilibet had written a letter, in the strictest confidence, to her couturier, Hardy Amies, to sketch out the outfits she would need for the visit. Even during the American trip, her beloved private secretary Martin Charteris (another who was sweetly and completely smitten!) had taken extra care that they had packed not merely mourning clothes – should those be needed – but also all the necessary accession documents. Now – it was simply a matter of waiting.

By the time they had returned from America, a lot of adjustments were necessary. For a start, there was a new government – the first purely Conservative Government since 1929. Mummie and Papa were thrilled. Mummie said that most British people were Tories at heart and felt happier with Tories in charge; but for Lilibet and Philip, matters were not so clear. Of course, old Winston was a war hero, but the Labour Party had brought in many wonderful things, especially a free Health Service for all.

'We must all be One Nation,' Philip said to her. 'The old class thing – it's over, sausage.'

Lilibet had known this forever, really. Grandpa England had known it, and when she was doing her ATS training in Windsor, she had known it. She had felt more in common with those fellow trainees, who called her 'Windsor', than she had with poor, gawky Alathea Fitzalan-Howard, Agatha Blimp, reading her historical romances and dreaming of some forgotten era of class superiority. Philip and Lilibet were going to have to be part of a New World. A new order of things. And Mummie! Darling Mummie had not really prepared her for it in the very least. She just knew it by instinct.

Winston did not know it. He was a darling, and they all loved him, of course they did, but with his orotund phrases, and his Victorian clothes, and his slurred speech and his shuffling gait, he was almost an embarrassment. Mummie said he was courtly in his manners, but to Lilibet, it felt like playacting, the over-frequent use of 'Your Majesties', the bowing and beaming. Mummie said the shlurred speech was because he had had strokes, but Margaret's reply to that was, 'Pull the other one, Mummie. The old boy's permanently plastered!'

That winter, she and Philip, with the King and the secretaries, prepared their visit to Australia. The plane would have to stop for refuelling, and the obvious place to do this would be Egypt. But events were a bit dicey in Egypt, apparently, so another African country would have to be found.

'Kenya!' had been Philip's suggestion.

'Go on,' growled Tommy Lascelles, suspiciously, showing that he needed convincing, and even Martin had looked quizzical.

'The Kenyan Government gave us a farm for a wedding present,' said Philip. 'It's on the edge of the jungle, with superb wildlife. We can see birds, apes, rhinos coming down to the water to drink. There's a hotel in the middle of it called Treetops. If we manage to time it right – three days either side of the new moon – we shall see the best night skies in the world.'

'Yes, Tommy?' Lilibet had asked, since Tommy had cleared his throat in that exaggerated manner, which Philip said was pure Jeeves.

'I hate to remind Your Royal Highnesses that Sagana Lodge, the farm which has been so generously donated to you, is in the middle of the Mau Mau territory. These people are—'

'People,' said Philip, interrupting any attempts by a courtier to be discourteous. 'And what is more, they are members of the Commonwealth.'

'It'll do us good to have a little break,' said Lilibet, 'before we go on to Australia.'

'Three weeks of cutting bloody tapes and ribbons and waving from the backs of cars,' Philip had said.

Poor Papa. They all had the usual family Christmas together at Sandringham, where Philip and Lilibet had managed to see the children a bit. (Again, the papers! Moaning about the fact that they had missed Charles's third birthday party – as if he could care – and besides they were in America at the time! One really felt that a diplomatic visit abroad was slightly more important than the birthday party of a little sprog, as Philip called him.) It had been wonderful to get to Sandringham, though: the cold Norfolk skies, the crispy frosty grass underfoot as one crunched to church, the wonderful silver altar installed by Queen Alexandra and a few days' shooting.

Later in January, the King had pretended to be well enough to take her and Philip to see *South Pacific* at the theatre. Judith Manning and Michael Barnett. They loved those American musicals, and for days afterwards, the songs stayed inside their heads. *You gotta have a dream . . . gotta have a DREAM come true.*

Papa really should not have come to London Airport to see them off, but he had insisted. Lilibet sometimes thought she would never get the image out of her head, of Papa in his greatcoat, standing there in the freezing February weather: doddery, deaf old Winston standing beside him, reeking of brandy at ten o'clock in the morning, holding his *Daily Mail* hat. 'What the devil's that ghastly hat Churchill's started to wear?' Grandpa England had asked the question all those years ago. And Grannie had replied, 'It's a hat specially designed for him by Lord Rothermere. A sort of crossbreed between a bowler and a trilby.' 'Why can't he wear a silk hat like every other fella?'

It was comforting that Bobo would be flying with them to Australia. Dearest, good Bobo, the most constant presence in her life, always. She had been closer to Bobo, really, than she had felt to Mummie, or even, if the truth were told, to Philip.

Standing there on the tarmac, with the cold winds blowing, the King managed to say, 'Look after the Princess for me, Bobo.'

And then they had all climbed aboard the aircraft, leaving the King and the Prime Minister waving.

14: Treetops

BOBO HAD ALWAYS BEEN THERE – before Crawfie, even. She would stay with her for sixty-seven years. When she was waking in the mornings, she always thought of Bobo, and expected it to be Bobo who would lift her up and hold her. When she was praying, Lilibet often thought of the little hymn Bobo would sing to her in the evenings – 'Nothing can thy power withstand, none can pluck me from thy hand.' It was like that with Bobo. While Bobo held her, she was safe.

And while the Queen slept, in the cradle of her old age, she was still rocked in the warmth of that safe, happy childhood.

It seemed, always, that the hour before she woke was the one when she slept most deeply, and on this night, the final hour was very deep. Such clouds of witness, so many people, crowded around her in the dark. Everywhere she went, crowds. She liked to joke that she had to be seen to be believed, and she must have been seen by millions. Philip said she must have shaken hands with more human beings than anyone else on the planet.

In that last, dark hour of night, she seemed to be processing, gliding through them, these multitudes: the crowds lining the Mall for the Jubilee; the milling crowd of MPs and peers as she was led in at all those State Openings; the crowds lining the walk down to the Castle, as she led the Knights of the Garter to their annual ceremony in St George's; the crowds around the paddock during Royal Ascot week.

And then, during the last couple of years, the strange solitude. Philip's funeral, with almost no one there, and one sitting alone. The empty rooms at Windsor. The empty walks and battlements when there were no tourists, no visitors, just the silence of this plague year. Of course, the crowds would return, and the royal round would begin again.

Now, in this strange dream procession in the black velvet of deepest sleep, one could not tell how one was being conveyed through the men and women, through the multitude of the years. That lovely hot feeling of stepping off a plane and knowing one was in Africa again! The Commonwealth – the common weal – before one's very eyes, peoples from every background, every walk of life, speaking so many different languages, all bound together in this great family. She had been right to fight for it, when so many of the politicians, the Little Englanders, had failed to see the point of it.

She remembered the face of Nelson Mandela. There was something in his eyes, and his smile, which made one absolutely confident that Good was stronger than Evil, that Love was stronger than Hate. She had felt humble in his presence. But there had been so many other wonderful African friends. Archbishop Tutu, so recently gone. Kwame Nkrumah! It still gave her pleasure to remember dancing with him, when she had been told so firmly by the pompous British politicians that she should not even *visit* Ghana. So many interesting African friends: Hastings Banda, Kenneth Kaunda, even Robert Mugabe – before he went off the rails, she'd had a lot of time for him.

As the mind-procession drifted, as she swept on in the cavalcade of dream, with faces flitting by – Harold Wilson, with his cheeky-chappy smile and his fondness, which she had never completely shared, for Gilbert and Sullivan, or rows upon rows of the showbiz stars, waiting to meet her at the Royal Variety performances in the London Palladium, or the devastated tear-splashed faces of bereaved parents in Aberfan or Lockerbie – she felt as if she were riding. Of course she was. She was not being driven in a car or a carriage, she was not flying, she was riding Betsy through the corridors of the aeons, through the paths of time. And here was Margaret, young and funny, making her laugh with imitations of friends; here was Mummie, giving off that reassuring combination of scent and gin, cheering on the Derby winner; here were the solemn faces of Field Marshals at the Cenotaph, and the overexcited schoolchildren, and the figures coming forward to be damed and knighted and OBE'd and MBE'd as appropriate band music played. Some of the memories were so awful – the Windsor Fire in '92, or the week when Diana died and one of the Household came to her and Philip in their sitting room in Balmoral and said, 'They are angry.' 'Who?' 'The People, ma'am.' And her only thought during those days had been to protect and cherish the poor little boys, William and Harry, and to keep them, as far as possible, from public gaze, whereas the papers, which she had not even had time to read, were running headlines such as 'SHOW US YOU CARE, MA'AM' and the crowds in the Mall were, according to reliable reports, distinctly hostile.

And yet never for a moment had she doubted that it was Destiny, the Hand of God, which led her.

And I said to the man who stood at
the gate of the year:
'Give me a light that I may tread safely
into the unknown.'
And he replied:
'Go out into the darkness and put your
hand into the Hand of God.
That shall be to you better than light
and safer than a known way.'
So I went forth, and finding the Hand of
God, trod gladly into the night.
And He led me towards the hills and the
breaking of day in the lone East.

In the warm darkness of bedclothes, in the blue-black dream of night, she remained safe and sound. The daybreak was coming. At the back of the old, rested, calm mind, there was knowledge that the daybreak would come, and she would know, immediately, who it would be who would wake her.

* * *

'Congratulations, sausage. You've caught your first Boji Plains nothobranch.'

In the Treetops Hotel, Philip was standing behind her, holding the rod, as the fish danced on the end of it.

'Beginner's luck!' she joked.

Despite their desperate worry about Papa – he had looked so frail and ill at the airport as he waved goodbye – it had been such a happy time, those few days in Kenya. They'd landed at Nairobi, and felt, rather than inhaled, that knowledge that they were – in Africa!

So many visits to Africa there'd been: to South Africa with Mummie and Papa on her twenty-first birthday, when she delivered her first broadcast to the Empire. And then, as the Empire transformed itself into a Commonwealth of free nations, so many more visits. She always felt strangely at home on African soil. Not surprising, really, since that was where the reign had begun – not in Balmoral, not in Sandringham, not in the Houses of Parliament, but perched up a giant fig tree in Nyeri, a hundred miles north of Nairobi, watching baboons through her binoculars.

There had been the usual official stuff at Nairobi Airport. A white man wearing a plumed hat had bowed to them as they came down the gangplank onto the tarmac.

'That man, the stuffed uniform in the feathers,' Philip had said when they were alone together again, in their bedroom that evening, 'he has no idea! None at all. I said

Philip was clambering up the rope ladder towards them on the observation deck. Their eyes met. Then she did not sort of know or almost know. She knew.

to him, "How many years before Kenya is independent?" and he looked at me as if I'd passed wind!'

'Oh, Philip.'

A car had taken them to engagements where they had shaken innumerable hands and read polite words from cards written out for them by the diplomats. And then there had been freedom!

The man in the plumed hat – the 'governor', Sir Philip Mitchell – had warned them against driving into the heart of Mau Mau territory. It was dangerous, and they would have to rough it. They were heading for Sagana Lodge, where they would get the chance to do some elephant-watching, some fishing and some photography. And then Philip's chum Mike Parker had the idea – they would go on to the Treetops Hotel.

'Not for the faint-hearted,' Mike told her.

'He means we'll have to crap in buckets,' Philip had quipped.

'Oh, but it will be an adventure,' she had said.

'We'll see so many animals . . .'

'And the great African heavens . . .'

Beginner's luck.

They were days of extraordinary peace. They were not His Royal Highness and Her Royal Highness. They were a man and a woman under the great inky-blue sky, where the stars in their multitudes sang a nightly miracle. From the balcony of the Treetops Hotel, they looked down on the jungle.

Mike was with her that dawn. Some other member of the party had called Philip away. Oddly enough, she did not guess why. She thought that the messenger who had driven down from Nairobi was simply bringing them the schedule for the next stage of their official business in Kenya. She and Mike stood on the observation deck looking at the dawn. It was the most wonderful dawn, starting a fiery red, and filling the whole sky eventually with gold. A new day. A new world. A new life.

And, just as the sun had risen and the colours of the trees were becoming clear, there was a stirring in the jungle treetops. Mighty as an archangel, a great crowned eagle emerged from the foliage and hovered in the sky, its huge wings spread out. It was so close they could see its very glossy, observant eyes, and its sharp beak. Mike said afterwards, he was afraid it might fly towards them and peck at them. Lilibet, though, had not been frightened. She was more interested in this visitation of the eagle than she was by the arrival of whoever-it-was from Nairobi who had asked to speak to Philip before six in the morning.

The moments in life of 'knowing'. On Bognor Beach, with Grandpa England, she had 'known' that he, and

Papa, and she, would carry something on, something given, something bigger than themselves. She had not needed to put this 'knowledge' into words. And then at Dartmouth, when Philip had followed the Royal Yacht in his rowing boat – she had 'known'. She was only thirteen, but she had known that he would be the man in her life.

And now, too, when the eagle rose out of the Kenyan jungle, she almost knew, sort of knew, that an extraordinary moment had arrived.

Philip was clambering up the rope ladder towards them on the observation deck.

Their eyes met. Then she did not sort of know, or almost know. She knew.

He took her arm, and led her quietly to their room.

When they emerged, Mike, and all the rest of the party, and the hotel staff, bowed. It had begun.

The Archbishop had lifted it high in the air, like a murder weapon –
it was the crown. And now he was lowering it upon her own head.
And she felt the weight of it.

Author's Note

DURING THE REIGN OF THE first Queen Elizabeth, Edmund Spenser, Sir Walter Raleigh and other poets celebrated the monarch, and what she symbolized, in such magnificent poems as *The Faerie Queene*.

Nearly forty years ago, when I was still a teacher of English Literature, I thought it would be fun to try to do the same for our Queen Elizabeth. I wrote a life of the Queen in verse, beginning with her birth, and ending with the accession to the throne on 6 February 1952. I entitled the poem *Lilibet* and published it anonymously. I wanted to see if it was possible to tell her story without reference to a modern author. It did not need my name on the title page.

Then, I was a young man, and now I am old. Our late Queen inspired verses now and again: most notably by Ted Hughes and by Philip Larkin, during her Silver Jubilee. As yet, however, there is no long poem. No *Gloriana*.

I should be shy at sharing my poem *Lilibet* with the world, although, when it was published, it had its admirers, including (no swanks) the Queen Mother who told me she had enjoyed it, and Sir John Betjeman, who at the time was Poet Laureate, said kind things about it.

Behind the poem *Lilibet* was the idea that the whole of the Queen's existence, and her devoted, symbolic, consecrated life of service, had been contained in her childhood and early youth, as chronicled by her governess Marion Crawford in a book entitled *The Little Princesses*.

With absolutely no personal knowledge of Her Majesty, I still believe this is the case, thinking that perhaps the reason she was such a stabilizing and constant figure on the world stage was that, inwardly, she never lost the ability to be the person she was aged nine – jigsaw-crazy, pony-mad, prayerful, dutiful, kind, a little distant, a little cold. The Royal Family were furious with 'Crawfie' for writing her book. I wonder if one reason for this was that it was so accurate: sugary certainly, sycophantic by modern standards, but with the photographic exactitude which can only be achieved by an unusually nosey observer without any imagination.

Perhaps this is merely a dream. I suspect, though, that even those closest to Her Majesty always found her an enigma. For that reason, perhaps only a poem, or a work of fiction, could capture her secret?

What I have written in these pages is not 'made up'. Nearly all of it is based on recorded events, conversations and incidents in Her Majesty's early life. It is, however, a work of the imagination. Everyone feels that there was something 'special' about the Queen, that she was unlike anyone else on this planet. She carried with her not merely her life experiences as an individual human being, but the history of her country, and of the Commonwealth, over the ninety-six years of her life.

Leabharlanna Poiblí Chathair Baile Átha Cliath

Dublin City Public Libraries

Lár Leabharlann Átha Cliath
Dublin Central Library
01-2228300